no other. The magic is still there, as is the love for this amazing story, only in a different way."
—*Six Blue Marbles*

Praise for Peter S. Beagle

"One of my favorite writers."
—Madeleine L'Engle, author of *A Wrinkle in Time*

"Peter S. Beagle illuminates with his own particular magic such commonplace matters as ghosts, unicorns, and werewolves. For years a loving readership has consulted him as an expert on those hearts' reasons that reason does not know."
—Ursula K. Le Guin, author of *A Wizard of Earthsea*

"Peter S. Beagle has both opulence of imagination and mastery of style."
—*New York Times Book Review*

"At his best, Peter S. Beagle outshines the moon, the sun, the stars, the entire galaxy."
—*Seattle Times*

"Peter Beagle deserves a seat at the table with the great masters of fantasy."
—Christopher Moore, author of *Lamb* and *The Serpent of Venice*

Praise for *The Last Unicorn*

"Comes alive and stays alive on bright intensity of imagination."
—*The New York Times Book Review*

"*The Last Unicorn* is the best book I have ever read. You need to read it. If you've already read it, you need to read it again."
—Patrick Rothfuss, author of *The Name of the Wind* and *The Wise Man's Fear*

"Almost as if it were the last fairy tale, come out of lonely hiding in the forests of childhood, *The Last Unicorn* is as full of enchantment as any of the favorite tales readers may choose to recall. . . . A delicate, sensitive, yet powerful rendering of all the intangibles that make a fairy tale unforgettable."
—*St. Louis Post-Dispatch*

"[*The Last Unicorn*] has inspired everything from *The Princess Bride* to *Stardust*."
—*Publishers Weekly*

Also by Peter S. Beagle

Fiction

A Fine and Private Place (1960)

The Last Unicorn (1968)

Lila the Werewolf (1969)

The Folk of the Air (1986)

The Innkeeper's Song (1993)

The Unicorn Sonata (1996)

Tamsin (1999)

A Dance for Emilia (2000)

The Last Unicorn: The Lost Version (2007)

Strange Roads (with Lisa Snellings-Clark, 2008)

Return (2010)

Summerlong (2016)

In Calabria (2017)

Short fiction collections

Giant Bones (1997)

The Rhinoceros Who Quoted Nietzsche and Other Odd Acquaintances (1997)

The Line Between (2006)

Your Friendly Neighborhood Magician: Songs and Early Poems (2006)

We Never Talk About My Brother (2009)

Mirror Kingdoms: The Best of Peter S. Beagle (2010)

Sleight of Hand (2011)

The Overneath (2017)

Nonfiction

I See By My Outfit (1965)

The California Feeling (with Michael Bry, 1969)

The Lady and Her Tiger (with Pat Derby, 1976)

The Garden of Earthly Delights (1982)

In the Presence of Elephants (with Pat Derby and Genaro Molina, 1995)

As editor

Peter S. Beagle's Immortal Unicorn (with Janet Berliner, 1995)

The Secret History of Fantasy (2010)

The Urban Fantasy Anthology (with Joe R. Lansdale, 2011)

The New Voices of Fantasy (with Jacob Weisman, 2017)

The Unicorn Anthology (with Jacob Weisman, forthcoming, 2019)

PETER S. BEAGLE

THE LAST UNICORN
The Lost Journey

Tachyon
San Francisco

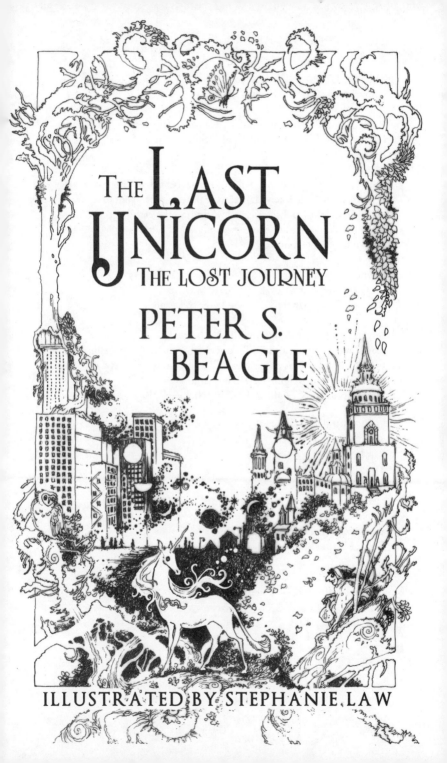

THE LAST UNICORN
THE LOST JOURNEY

PETER S. BEAGLE

ILLUSTRATED BY STEPHANIE LAW

Tachyon Publications LLC
1459 18th Street #139
San Francisco, CA 94107
415.285.5615
www.tachyonpublications.com
tachyon@tachyonpublications.com

Series Editor: Jacob Weisman
Project Editor: Jill Roberts

Print ISBN: 978-1-61696-308-8
Limited Edition ISBN: 978-1-61696-318-7

First Edition: 2018
9 8 7 6 5 4 3 2 1

Printed in Canada

For Jon Gunnar Howe,
the brightest kid in Santa Cruz High.
I miss you, my friend.

Contents

Introduction
PATRICK ROTHFUSS

The Last Unicorn is my favorite book. It has been for years. I recommend it relentlessly. I wax rhapsodic about it on panels, and I've been known to hand-sell it to other customers when I'm at a bookstore. (To frequently bewildered folk, who often assume that I work there.)

It is a marvelous book. And that's not just my personal fondness speaking. The simple truth of the matter is that *The Last Unicorn* is one of the cornerstones of fantasy literature.

In that context, what you're holding in your hands is an exceedingly remarkable thing. A rarity of the highest degree. It's the first draft of a book ·

that would be rewritten, published, and go on to change the landscape of fantasy.

As a lover of this book, I'm fascinated. It's like reading an early draft of *The Lord of the Rings* where Tom Bombadil shows up at Bilbo's door instead of Gandalf. Or like seeing the original pencil sketches for Van Gogh's *The Starry Night*. Early on, back when he was thinking of putting a hot air balloon in there. . . .

As a writer of fantasy, I'm flabbergasted. I revise constantly. Not just structure and scene, I tweak sentences and phrases and individual words. I endlessly massage my language, dozens and hundreds of revisions as I strive to make my phrasing clear and crisp. Sharp and sweet. Wondrous and strange.

But reading this first draft . . . huge chunks of it are in no way rough. They have, apparently, sprung fully-formed from the mind of twenty-year-old Peter. Lovely, sweet language. Pristine scenes. They needed no revising, and they received none. It's stupefying, honestly. And I don't know if I should be filled with wonder or despair.

As an aficionado of the fantasy genre, I am a little wistful. Peter made the right call in his changes.

Changes needed to be made. The story needed to follow the unicorn, so some characters needed to be pruned.

But still, I read this book, and I wonder at what might have been. . . .

Preface:
HOW TO RECOGNIZE MAGIC WHEN YOU SEE IT

CARRIE VAUGHN

For me, the magical thing about *The Last Unicorn* —I mean besides the language, the characters, the dream-like qualities, the heart-stopping beauty of its world and poignancy of its story, and well, everything—is how it's different every time I read it. The first time I read it I absolutely wanted to be a unicorn, or a princess who had been a unicorn, or something equally painfully beautiful and magical. The most recent time I read it, my heart jumped a bit when I realized I was, in fact, Molly Grue— and that I was perfectly all right with being Molly Grue. She's got her feet in both worlds. Easy to be so dazzled by the unicorn you forget about Molly, and that would be a mistake. Molly teaches us that it's never too late to have real magic enter your life. You just have to make sure you never lose the trick of recognizing it.

Like many of my generation (Generation X, which is said to be cynical, but I think we're cynical in the same way Molly is cynical—we so desperately want to believe but instead we so often run into Captain Cullys and King Haggards and we're getting old and we got tired. But by God we see the unicorn for what she is.), my first exposure to *The Last Unicorn* was through the ethereal animated film. Could anything be so delicate as the unicorn, or so awful as the Bull? It's haunting. I like the film mostly because it led me to the book, which in turn led me to the rest of Peter Beagle's writing.

The Last Unicorn: The Lost Journey is wonderful for the seeds it plants. It's not the book I know, but the seed of it. It's about magic leaving the world— because modernity is shoving it out. It's about people not seeing magic even when looking right at it. Here, when the unicorn declares that she would make a good human being, it's easy to stumble on that line and think, oh dear, oh no. The seed was there all along, wasn't it?

This journey is more philosophy and less story than the version I know, and I wonder if the philosophy had to get laid down first and incubate a bit before the story could grow out of it. Peter wrote the philosophy of it as a young man, and the story after telling stories to his own children, in his own account of the book's evolution. Seems perfectly natural to me.

Some writers' work inspires me to be better, to strive, to pick apart how they do what they do and try to apply the lessons to my own writing. Peter's work, I just enjoy. I fall into it. I always feel better after reading it, and that's a gift. It's like recognizing magic, which was always right there for us.

I

The unicorn lived in a lilac wood, and she lived all alone. She was very old, though she did not know it, and she was no longer the careless color of sea foam, but rather the color of snow falling on a moonlit night. But her eyes were still clear and unwearied, and she still moved like a shadow on the sea.

She did not look anything like a horned horse, as unicorns are often pictured, being smaller and cloven-hoofed, and possessing that oldest, wildest grace that horses have never had, that deer have only in a shy, thin imitation and goats in dancing mockery. Her neck was long and slender, making her head seem smaller than it was, and the mane

1

that fell almost to the middle of her back was as soft as dandelion fluff and as fine as cirrus. She had pointed ears and thin legs, with feathers of white hair at the ankles; and the long horn above her eyes shone and shivered with its own seashell light even in the deepest midnight. She had killed dragons with it, and healed a king whose poisoned wound would not close, and knocked down ripe chestnuts for bear cubs.

Unicorns are immortal. It is their nature to live alone in one place: usually a forest where there is a pool clear enough for them to see themselves— for they are a little vain, knowing themselves to be the most beautiful creatures in all the world, and magic besides. They mate very rarely, and no place is more enchanted than one where a unicorn has been born. The last time she had seen another unicorn the young virgins who still came seeking her now and then had called to her in a different tongue; but then, she had no idea of months and years and centuries, or even of seasons. It was always spring in her forest, because she lived there, and she wandered all day among the great beech trees, keeping watch over the animals that lived in the ground and under bushes, in nests and caves, earths and treetops. Generation after generation, wolves and rabbits alike, they hunted and loved and had children and died, and as the unicorn did none of these things, she never grew tired of watching them.

One morning, the wind bore her an oily, sulphurous reek that sent her nostrils flaring with the oldest terror of all her kind. The dragon-smell never leaves you, having once touched your throat; not in a hundred years, not in five hundred. Faint on the wind from the other side of the forest, it hurt the unicorn's eyes, and she shivered and stamped in fear. The hatred between dragons and unicorns goes a long way back, to the time when the first unicorn wandered into a world full of dragons, and there has never been peace between them, nor ever will be. Wherever they are, and whenever, when they meet they must fight, and one of them always dies.

The unicorn had killed three dragons in her life, but she was always afraid, and she always ran away when the beasts were dead. She was afraid now, but she knew her duty, and she raced through the forest like sunlight, leaping over brooks and bushes, feeling vines and creepers tangling in her mane and around her horn. The dragon-smell grew stronger, filling her nostrils like smoke, until at last she burst into a clearing where the dragon crouched, hissing fire. Rearing on her hind legs, her horn glowing with its own deep fires, she cried out the old and terrible challenge of unicorn to dragon. The cry had not been heard in her forest in the lifetime of any other animal, and it changed the courses of three streams, turned every golden eagle in the forest white, and made an owl who was writing his autobiography forget his own name for two weeks.

Considering that it had been a century since she had made any sound at all, the unicorn was frankly pleased with her own battle music. She almost wished to be the dragon, the better to hear herself. "Come and fight with me, dragon!" she cried. "Come and fight, and be beautiful, and die!" But the dragon only looked at her, twitched his black lips once or twice, and began to cry.

"Oh, that's all," he whispered quietly. "Oh, my scaly tail, that is absolutely all." He cried very softly, with his eyes closed and his head lowered, but his tears splashed his feeble fires out with a smell like gunpowder. "Come and fight, come and fight," he mumbled. "A dragon comes crawling home half-dead, and the first thing he hears is come and fight, come and fight. I'm tired, my stomach hurts, I have a headache—go away and leave me alone. Fighting all the time, all the time." He sniffled like a distant hurricane, and licked forlornly at his tears with his forked tongue.

The unicorn came down on all four feet with a thud and stared at the dragon in complete bewilderment. The only tears she had ever seen were those of lonely young girls. She had never imagined that anything else in the world wept. Nothing in her long life prepared her to deal with a weeping dragon. She cleared her throat and said hesitantly, "What's the matter? Are you unhappy?"

"No, I'm fine," the dragon muttered bitterly. "I'm just lovely, I am. Jolliest dragon in the whole world, that's me." His tears were beginning to form an emerald-green puddle around his front paws, and the unicorn danced daintily back a few paces. "If you knew where I've been!" he wept. "If you'd seen the things I've seen! You wouldn't be going around picking fights then, I can tell you."

He was a larger dragon than the unicorn had first thought, and almost as old as herself, for the scales on his body were a dull greenish-black, and his claws were blunt with age, no sharper than a turtle's. The long, low purple crest running along his back from his ears to his tail-tip—a dragon's joy—was torn in several places, and lay limp and prideless. The poisonous spikes at the end of his tail were all broken off short, and he wheezed and coughed and rattled when he breathed out his damp ashes, as though he were all rusty inside. He rolled in his own tears and wailed until both the unicorn's fear and her patience were quite vanished.

"Oh, do stop crying, for heaven's sake," she told him snappily. "Haven't you any shame? What would all the other dragons think if they saw you now?"

Dragons have much more sense of family than unicorns do, but the unicorn's appeal only made the old dragon grin like a broken piano through his green tears. "They're all crying," he said, "every one. Right now, every dragon in the world is lying down and howling with frustration. Listen to the rain some time, you'll hear them." The unicorn stared at him without understanding, and he became equally impatient with her. "Or doesn't it ever rain around here anymore?" he demanded. "Don't you ever go anywhere, don't you ever look around you? Don't you know what's happening in the world?"

The unicorn shook her head. "I never travel," she replied, as mildly as if she were speaking to another unicorn.

"I never travel," the dragon mimicked her. "Every time I look at one of you people, I have to bite something." He snorted damply. "Well, I'm done traveling," he said. "No more. I just want to lie down

somewhere, in a nice hole in the riverbank, nice and damp and cool. Unless you really want to kill me here. I don't much care. I'd just as soon get killed by a galloping anachronism as on that road I followed here." His eyes squeezed shut, as if he were about to start crying again. "Oh, that road," he mourned, "that terrible black road."

"The road to my forest," the unicorn said, "is wide and white as wings. I haven't been on it in some time, but I remember that I always liked the little dusty sound it made under my feet. No one comes to see me over that road anymore, but it is still there, just as it was, wide and good to walk on."

"Sweet and foolish lady," the dragon answered her, "the road to your forest is made of black iron, and on it, all day and all night, the coaches run and roar, and flash yellow lights till they drive you mad, and yell like sea-demons. They're bigger than I am, some of them, and they run faster than you ever dreamed of running." Very gingerly he twitched the battered tip of his tail. "One of them ran over my tail," he said. "Can you imagine what that was like for me, to be run over by a coach?" He sniffled, rubbed his nose on his forepaw, and went on. "The coachman told me it was my fault. He said I was going too slowly. Oh, I ate him up, but it didn't make me feel any better. It was because I was afraid of the coach, and I knew it, inside. And the road hurt my feet so. I kept looking for a better road, someplace quiet and sandy, with children playing in puddles, and a few sheep here and there, but I couldn't find any of those. I think all the roads are like that one now."

"So my white road is gone," the unicorn said softly. "Well, why should I be surprised?" Nevertheless, she felt a little sad, and she wished the dragon had not told her. "So long as there is still a road," she said. "But tell me about the city, the city where the kings lived. Is the city gone too?"

"What do you care about the city?" the dragon jeered at her. "Little white soul, you've never once set foot in any city, not in all your life. What difference would it make to you if the kings' city had turned to straw yesterday morning, and been eaten down by donkeys?"

"I know all about the city," the unicorn answered. "I have always known about the city, but I don't know how I know. It shines in my head the way I know the ocean shines, and I've never seen the ocean, either." Her light feet were almost dancing with impatience. "Tell me about the city," she said. "Do the princes still walk through the streets at noon, very slowly, and is the city still full of birds?"

"What the city is full of, mostly," replied the dragon, "is policemen." He moaned against his broken claws and began to shiver all over. "Policemen," he said. "I don't suppose you happen to see policemen in your head, but believe me, they outnumber the birds. Oh, my teeth—they come up to you and say, uh, you just passing through here or what, and you say, oh, I'm going right on through, sir, just as fast as my four old feet can carry me. And he says, because you look sort of strange, and you say, yes, I know, lovely sir, my fault entirely, and I'll take a bath just as soon as I can. And you start to go away from there, and he puts up his hand and says, well, just to make sure about things, how about you show me your license? And you get all excited, and you start to feel a little bit incineratory where all the fire is, and you say, what license? Can't you see I'm a dragon? And he says, well, maybe that's what you are where you come from, but in this town you're a vehicle, and I'm asking to see your license. Because we got an ordinance in this town about vehicles more than twenty-nine feet long," the dragon said miserably.

"And then you say, oh, I can't stand this, and you eat him up. And that's a mistake, that is a tactical error. Boy, do they throw the book at you for eating up a policeman. Especially if it's Sunday. They have an ordinance about that, too."

"Yes, but the princes," the unicorn insisted. "There were princes in the city, I know there were."

"Not anymore," the dragon said. "Just policemen."

"What are policemen to me? Tell me about the people, then, if there are no princes. I used to dream that they were gentle and happy in that city—are they still?"

"That I wouldn't know," the dragon answered indifferently. "But they taste terrible. They taste like clocks and coal oil. And the children are bitter as silver—now, that surprised me. The children used to be the best eating in the world, better than antelope, better than wild geese, but now I just can't bring myself to eat another one of them. Oh, it's been dogs and cats and mangy little squirrels for weeks now—and when you think how I used to dine off steamed knight, knight on the half-shell, broiled in his own armor with all the natural juices—excuse me, I'm going to cry again."

The unicorn had almost forgotten that she was

talking to a dragon. Now she backed away from him, the hairs of her mane flaring as if the wind were passing over her. "Go away," she said. "You may stay in my forest, but go away now."

"Much thanks for such a sanctuary." The dragon sneered out the old courtly words, and began to slither past her into the woods, groaning with the effort of lifting his belly off the ground. "My back's killing me," he grumbled. "Aches all the time, right there, behind the hump. The funny thing is, all the dragons I've met in the last hundred years had back trouble. My cousin says it's chronic, has to do with the new air. He says, after a while you start to shrink, and then it doesn't hurt so much. The smaller you are, the less it hurts. My cousin says that's why there aren't many of us left. We all just small away to nothing. Funny, isn't it? Makes you feel lonely, if you're used to having a lot of dragons around."

"I don't understand," the unicorn said. She hated and feared all dragons, but she could not imagine a world without them. That really does make me feel lonely, she thought. How strange, how ridiculous. "What about unicorns?" she asked hesitantly. "Did you see any unicorns, on the road or in the city?"

Then the dragon swung his long neck at her like

a whip, and grinned with all his rusty teeth showing. "I didn't see any unicorns anywhere," he answered. "That's a fact. I didn't see a single one." His eyes were glowing red-yellow, like hunter's moons.

"None?" The unicorn stood very still. "No unicorns at all?"

"Not a one," answered the dragon, quite cheerful now. "Neither did my cousin. He says there isn't one of them left. We dwindle, he says, but they just vanish. Of course, he hadn't had the pleasure."

"I don't believe you," she said. She felt a slow coldness spreading through her. "Why should all the unicorns disappear?"

"Who needs them?" the dragon grunted. "I tell you truly, I don't much like this time on the earth. It's a bad time for dragons. But it's no time at all for unicorns, and that's something, anyway." He waved his tail at her, almost jauntily. "Enjoy your singularity while you can," he said. "You're one myth that was always more trouble than it was worth."

Waving his tail had been a mistake. It seemed to upset his internal equilibrium. He gulped and blinked, and the momentary ferocity in his eyes was replaced by simple discomfort. "Excuse me," he whispered. "I have to lie down." He dragged himself off into the forest, hiccupping and groaning, and she could hear him being miserable in the underbrush for a long time after he was out of sight.

The unicorn stood where she was and said, *I am the only unicorn there is* to herself, to hear how it sounded.

That can't be, she thought. She had never minded being alone, never seeing another unicorn, because she had always known that there were others like her in the world, and a unicorn needs no more than that for company. "But I would know if all the others were gone. I'd be gone too. Nothing can happen to them that does not happen to me."

Her own voice frightened her and made her want to be running. She moved along the dark paths of her forest, swift and shining, passing through sudden clearings unbearably brilliant with grass or soft with shadow, aware of everything around her, from the weeds that brushed her ankles to insect-quick flickers of blue and silver as the wind lifted the leaves. "Oh, I could never leave this, I never could, not if I really were the only unicorn in the world. I know how to live here, I know how everything smells, and tastes, and is. What could I ever search for in the world, except this again?"

But when she stopped running at last and stood still, listening to crows and a quarrel of squirrels over her head, she wondered, but suppose they are hiding together, somewhere far away? What if they are hiding and waiting for me?

From that first moment of doubt, there was no peace for her; from the time she first imagined leaving her forest, she could not stand in one place without wanting to be somewhere else. She trotted up and down beside her pool, restless and unhappy. Unicorns are not meant to make choices. She said no, and yes, and no again, day and night, and for the first time she began to feel the minutes crawling over her like worms. "I will not go. Because men have seen no unicorns for a while does not mean they have all vanished. Even if it were true, I would not go. I live here."

Sleep provided no respite, but left her exhausted, as though she were already journeying, while struggling to turn back. She dreamed often, which is unusual for a unicorn, but her dreams offered only confusion and a heartsickness that was strange to her. "I will not go. There is no need, there cannot be a need. No."

But at last she woke up in the middle of one

warm night and said, "Yes, but now." She hurried through her forest, trying to look at nothing and smell nothing, trying not to feel her earth under her cloven hoofs. The animals who move in the dark, the owls and the foxes and the deer, raised their heads as she passed by, but she would not look at them. I must go quickly, she thought, and come back as soon as I can. Maybe I won't have to go very far. But whether I find the others or not, I will come back very soon, as soon as I can.

Under the moon, the road that ran from the edge of her forest gleamed like water, but when she stepped out onto it, away from the trees, she felt how hard it was, and how long. She almost turned back then; but instead she took a deep breath of the woods air that still drifted to her, and held it in her mouth like a flower, as long as she could.

II

The long road hurried to nowhere and had no end. It ran through villages and small towns, flat country and mountains, stony barrens and meadows springing out of stones, but it belonged to none of these, and it never rested anywhere. It rushed the unicorn along, tugging at her feet like the tide, fretting at her, never letting her be quiet and listen to the air, as she was used to do. Her eyes were always full of dust, and her mane was stiff and heavy with dirt.

Time had always passed her by in her forest, but now it was she who passed through time as she traveled. The colors of the trees changed, and the animals along the way grew heavy coats and lost them again; the clouds crept or hurried before the changing winds, and were pink and gold in the sun or livid with storm. Wherever she went, she searched for her people, but she found no trace of them, and in all the tongues she heard spoken along the road there was not even a word for them anymore.

Early one morning, about to turn off the road to sleep, she saw an old couple hoeing and raking in their small garden. Knowing that she should hide, she stood still instead and watched them work, until they straightened as one and saw her. The woman was tall and gaunt, with eyes and skin of the same slaty gray. She said in a low voice, "Martin. Martin, look at that."

The man's mouth dropped open as he stared at the unicorn. He was fat, and his cheeks jumped with every step he took. "Oh," he said. "Oh, she's beautiful."

When he tugged off his belt, made a loop in it, and moved clumsily toward her, the unicorn was more pleased than frightened. The man knew what she was, and what he himself was for: to hoe turnips and pursue something that shone and could run faster than he could. She sidestepped his first lunge as lightly as though the wind of it had blown her out of his reach. "I have been hunted with bells and banners in my time," she told him. "Men knew that the only way to hunt me was to make the chase so wondrous that I would come near to see it. And even so, I was never once captured."

"Martin, be careful!" the woman called anxiously. "Remember your bad knees."

"Get around behind her, then," he snapped, picking himself up. "Steady now, you pretty thing. . . . To the *left*, woman!"

"I've never really understood," the unicorn mused, "what you dream of doing with me, once you've caught me." The man leaped again, and she slipped away from him like rain. "I don't think you know yourselves," she said.

The woman was moving timidly up on her left, whispering, "Pretty, pretty—*here*, pretty," as though she were calling chickens. The unicorn sidestepped without even looking at her.

"Ah, steady, steady, easy now." The man's sweating face was striped with dirt, and he could hardly get his breath. "Sweet," he gasped. "You sweet little mare."

"*Mare?*" The unicorn trumpeted the word so shrilly that the man took a step backward, and the woman clapped her hands to her ears. "Mare?" she demanded. "I, a horse? Is that what you take me for? Is that what you see?"

"Martin, she's wild, be *careful!*" The woman tugged at her husband's arm. "Come away, she's wild!"

"Good horse," the fat man panted. He shook loose from his wife's grip, wiping his face. "Curry you up, clean you off, you'll be the sweetest old mare anywhere." He reached out with the belt again. "Take you to the fair," he said. "Come on, horse."

"A horse," the unicorn said. "That's what you were trying to capture. A white mare with her mane full of burrs." As the man approached her, she hooked her horn through the belt, jerked it out of his grasp, and hurled it at the woman, making her scream and jump out of the way. "A horse, am I?" she snorted. "A horse, indeed!"

For a moment the man was very close to her, and her great eyes stared into his own, which were small and tired and amazed. Then she turned and bolted up the road, no longer caring about being seen by men, or that the black road hurt her feet, galloping so swiftly that the few men who did see her exclaimed, "Boy, that's some horse! Boy, that's a racehorse!" Watching her go, the fat man said quietly to his wife, "That's an Arab horse. I was on a ship with an Arab horse once."

She ran until the sight of trees and soft grass by the roadside reminded her that she was tired and hungry. A little boy was sitting under the biggest tree of all, playing with the earth, and for no reason that she could think of, the unicorn stopped there and stood still, looking down at him. He was a very little boy, three or four years old, and he had dark hair and a perfectly round face. One of his feet was bare, and his overall straps kept sliding down his shoulders. He waved his hands at the unicorn and said, "Horse."

"Child," the unicorn said wearily, "I am not a horse. I am a unicorn, perhaps the last one in the world, and there was a time when even a boy your age would know me, and know enough to do me honor instead of sitting there drawing pictures in the dust." But the little boy reached imperiously out for her, and she let her legs fold under her and sank down beside him. The boy promptly plunged his grubby hands into her mane, half-stroking, half-tugging. A great lassitude overcame her then: not sleep, exactly, but a kind of comfortingly disjointed reverie, crowding her ancient mind with smoky shadows out of lost times. There were kings of men in those shadows, and creatures like and unlike herself—royalty of another, wilder sort—and the world that had contained them, itself faintest and farthest of all. The unicorn dozed under the tree, and the little boy sang quietly to himself in a language as meaningless as her memories.

Once—once only—it seemed to her that she had abandoned her quest and returned to her forest, to be welcomed joyously by every twig and leaf and blade of grass, by every beast and bird, from the least to the greatest; by the wind that knew her and that carried the word and the scent and the old promise of her to . . . to a small and very dirty boy who crooned shrill gibberish to her and wound grasses around her horn. Now and then she almost dreamed of princes riding through her forest, hunting strange beast-birds, and of girls who came shyly, holding out golden bridles. But each time she started out of her half-sleep, there was only the black road and the swift coaches rushing by, and the little boy's hand in her mane. She knew that she must start on her way soon, but she did not want to, and she stayed as long as she could.

"Grass is all right," she said to the boy, because he kept shoving it into her mouth, "but what I would really like is a flower, a daisy or a violet." Then she told herself, don't be foolish. The child can't hear you, none of these people can. But the boy promptly got up, walked a little way from the tree, and came back to her with a bunch of violets. He sat down next to her again and fed her the violets one by one. Sometimes he even ate one himself.

"They taste good, don't they?" said the unicorn, before she suddenly realized that the little boy had understood what she had said to him. "Can you hear me?" she demanded. "Can you speak to me? Do you know what I am?"

"Horse," the boy answered calmly, and he would not say another word until they had eaten all the violets. Then he looked over the unicorn's head and said "Mommy," and the unicorn turned and saw a woman walking down the road towards them. She heard her calling to the boy.

"Child," the unicorn said, "Child, I have nothing to give you, but if you can speak to me, if you can tell me where my people are hiding, I will think of you when there is no one left in the world to remember your name." Then, realizing that this was nothing to say to a child, she added, "And I will take you for a ride on my back whenever you wish." But the little boy was trying to find out if her horn came off, and his mother was shouting at him to get away from that horse because it had bugs.

"Why won't you talk to me?" the unicorn cried desperately. She got to her feet and stared down at the boy, who clung to her leg, trying to hide from his mother. At the unicorn's words, he raised his face to her and smiled, all shiny teeth and pink gums and pink, catty tongue. Quite clearly, he said to her, "What do you want from me? I can't even talk like people yet."

Then his mother dragged him away in a scurry of skirts and a waggling of fingers, telling him what would happen to him the next time he lost his good shoes and played with horses. He waved back at the unicorn, calling "Horse, horse," until they were out of sight.

The unicorn took up her journey again, traveling slowly, unsure of her way. The black road led her through mountains and across water, and she followed it patiently, although she was always a little tired. She had no idea how long she had been walking, nor of where she had been. Sometimes the air smelled of smoke and sometimes of fresh-cut hay. But to the unicorn it was all only night and day and night again.

Then one afternoon the butterfly wobbled out of a breeze and lit on the tip of her horn. He was velvet all over, dark and dusty looking, with golden spots on his wings, and he was as thin as a flower petal. Dancing along her horn, he saluted her with

his curling feelers and said, "I am a roving gambler. How do you do?"

The unicorn laughed for the first time in her travels. "Butterfly, what are you doing out in such a windy day?" she asked him. "You'll catch cold and die long before your time."

"Death takes what man would keep," said the butterfly, "and leaves what man would lose. Blow, wind, and crack your cheeks. I warm my hands before the fire of life and get four-way relief." He flamed like a scrap of sunset at the tip of her horn.

"Do you know what I am, butterfly?" the unicorn asked hopefully, and he replied, "Excellent well, you're a fishmonger. You're my everything, you are my sunshine, you are old and gray and full of sleep, you're my pickle-face, consumptive Mary Jane." He paused, fluttering his wings against the wind, and added conversationally, "your name is a golden bell hung in my heart. I would break my body to pieces to call you once by your name."

"Say my name, then," the unicorn urged him. "If you know my name, tell it to me." She felt a shivering inside herself, as fragile as the butterfly's wings. "Tell me my name," she said.

"Rumpelstiltskin," the butterfly answered happily.

"Gotcha! You don't get no medal." He jigged and twinkled on her horn, singing "Won't you come home, Bill Bailey, won't you come home? The ships in the meadow, the ethan is frome. Buckle down Winsocki, go and catch a falling star. Clay lies still, but blood's a rover. Please show me the way to the gentleman's room." His eyes were gleaming scarlet in the glow of the unicorn's horn.

She sighed and plodded on, more amused than disappointed. It serves you right, she told herself. You know better than to expect a butterfly to know your name. All they know are songs and poetry and anything else they hear. They mean well, but they can't keep things straight. And why should they? The butterfly swaggered before her eyes, singing "One, two, three o'lairy," as he whirled; chanting, "Oh, oh, Jim. See the pussycat! Run, pussycat, run! This would be a marvelous exhibition if it had less paintings. And now, in asking ourselves what lies ahead for the Cambodians, a host of furious fancies whereof I am commander will be on sale for three days only at bargain summer prices. Look down, looked down that lonesome road, look out dere, old Kemo-sabe, get him in the gun hand, like always, oh, the horror, the horror, my name is Peggy and my husband's name is McNamara and we live on vitamin C. I can dance with a shoe-nail in my heel and never a sign of the pain reveal, and aroint thee, witch, aroint thee, I love you, I love you, indeed and truly you've chosen a bad place to be lame in, willow, willow, willow." His voice tinkled in the unicorn's head, like little silver hands.

He traveled with her for the rest of the waning day, but when the sun was beginning to sink, he flew off her horn and hovered in the air before her. "I must take the A train," he said politely. Against the rosy clouds she could see that his velvet wings were ribbed with delicate black veins.

"Farewell," she said. "I have enjoyed your songs," which was the best way she could think of to part from a butterfly. But instead of leaving her, he fluttered above her head, looking suddenly less dashing and a little uneasy in the blue evening air. "Fly away," she urged him. "It's too cold for you to be out." But the butterfly still lingered, humming to himself.

"They ride that horse you call the Macedonai," he intoned absentmindedly; and then, very clearly, "Unicorn. Old French, *unicorne*. Latin, *unicornis*. My horn shall be exalted, like the horn of the unicorn. Oh, I am a cook and a captain bold and the mate of the *Nancy* brig. Has anybody here seen Kelly?" He strutted joyously in the air, and the first fireflies blinked around him in wonder and grave doubt.

The unicorn was so startled and so happy to hear her name spoken at last that she overlooked the remark about the horse. "Oh, you do know me!" she cried, and the breath of her delight blew the butterfly twenty feet away. When he came scrambling back to her, she pleaded, "Butterfly, if you really know what I am, tell me if you have ever seen anyone like me, tell me which way I must go to find them." She did not dare to hope, but she hoped anyway.

"Butterfly, butterfly, where shall I hide?" he sang in the fading light. "Biblical: a two-horned animal called *reem* in Hebrew. A. V. Deuteronomy xxxiii, 17. Hi-diddle-dee, bats in the belfry, jolly old Dr. Freud." He shook his head impatiently and recited, "His firstling bull has majesty, and his horns are the horns of a wild ox. With them he shall push the peoples, all of them, to the ends of the earth. Christ, that my love were in my arms, and I in my bed again." He rested on the unicorn's horn for a brief moment, and she could feel him trembling.

"Yes," she said, "but I want to know about my

own people." She was suddenly almost angry at something she could not name. "I hoped to find the princes again," she said to the butterfly, "and a jade city where griffins walked on the walls and there were great, soft swans like clouds on the river, but that time is gone. All I want now is to know that there are other unicorns somewhere in the world. Butterfly, tell me that there are still others like me, and I will believe you and go home to my forest." I have been away so long, she thought, and I said that I would come back soon.

"Over the mountains of the moon," the butterfly answered, "down the Valley of the Shadow, ride, boldly ride." Then he stopped suddenly and said in a strange voice, "No, no, listen, don't listen to me, listen. You can find your people, if you are brave. They passed through all the cities long ago, and the black road ran close behind them and covered their footprints. Now they live in a valley where the wild flowers nod. No. Now they live in a desert at the end of the road, and they hear people coming a long way off, and run. Nobody knows where they are, except the butterflies. Butterflies know everything." He began to sing, "Follow me down. Follow me down. Follow me down. Follow me down," but he wriggled all over, like a tiny jeweled fish, and said, "No, no, listen quickly. Get off the road, get off the road, for you'll never get to the end of it by following it. In the middle of the woods, at the bottom of a ravine, there is a frozen-custard stand. The owner lives under a pile of leaves, and that's how you'll know he's there. You must ask him to show you the way, or he'll be angry, but go on before he has time to answer. Listen to me. Whenever you see two roads, and you always will, take the one to the right, although it won't make any difference. Keep the sound of the stream on your left, unless there's nothing you can do about it. Keep the sun over your left shoulder and the moon over your right, because it's bad luck the other way. When there is no moon, follow the stars and see what it gets you. Don't play with matches. Travel as long as you can, and if you come to a great desert with sand the color of honey, see if your people are there. Let nothing you dismay, but don't be half-safe." His body seemed to be curling with exhaustion, but his eyes gleamed brighter than the fireflies.

"Thank you," the unicorn said doubtfully. "I will do everything just as you have told me, I suppose."

"Exactly, exactly, to the letter, or your wishes

won't come true. Don't mess around with the wrath of a butterfly." He swooped close to her ear, jaunty and eager as if they had just met, and added, "About butterflies. Let me tell you one more thing about butterflies, butterflaps, butterflutters. A thing." The unicorn lifted her head to hear him.

"We're all crazy," the butterfly laughed, "all of us, all us butterflies. Mad, fond, out of our minds, unstable. How could we be butterflies and not be crazy? Look at the way we fly, all sideways. You have to be bats to fly like a butterfly. Millions of us, all watching each other flying sideways. Oh, we're all crazy, and we get crazier, just watching." His wings brushed against the unicorn's skin so fleetingly that it was like a touch remembered from a long time ago. "I have nightmares about crawling around on the ground," he sang. "The little dogs, Tray, Blanche, Sue, they bark at me, the little snakes, they hiss at me, the beggars are coming to town. Then, at last, came the clams."

For a moment more he danced in the dust before her; then he shivered away into the violet shadows by the roadside, chanting defiantly, "It's you or me, moth! Hand to hand to hand to hand to hand. . . ." The last the unicorn saw of him was a tiny skittering between the trees, and her eyes might have deceived her, for the night was full of wings.

At least he did recognize me, she thought sadly. That means something. But she answered herself, no, that means nothing at all, except that somebody once made up a song about unicorns, or a poem. I didn't know butterflies were mad. Is it just this place that makes them so, or were they always mad? I should notice them more, things like butterflies, the ones who have no time. I see so little. I wonder what a butterfly would see if he could live as long as I have.

She walked on slowly, and the night drew close about her. The sky was low and almost pure black, save for one spot of yellowing silver where the moon seemed to pace forever behind the thick clouds. Now and then, one of the swift coaches hissed by, shoving the night to one side in a glare of light that sent its shadow sliding before and behind it and made the trees look gaunt as bones; but there was always something ridiculous and frightened about the two little red lights hurrying away down the road from the returning darkness, darker than before. The night was very still. There had been a few crickets, but they stopped after awhile, one by one, as though the loneliness of their own piping had grown too heavy for them to bear. There were no fireflies now.

Should I turn off the road? the unicorn wondered. The butterfly was mad, yes, but perhaps he really was trying to tell me how to find my people. And I hate this road. I think I will always feel it under my feet, like something I've stepped in and can't scrape off. Yet she delayed turning either to the steep woods on her right or to the slope on her left, and she knew that it had very little to do with the butterfly's dizzying advice. The night seemed to be stroking her with cold, damp fingers, and she was suddenly glad and greedy of her skin that held the night away from her bones, and of the feathery sound of her own hooves.

Something moves, she thought, something is up and walking in the night, and I almost remember what it is. The unicorn saw some things, the most important things, by smell, and there was an odor abroad on the thick air that was far older than the dragon-scent, and far more terrifying. Lightning smells like that, or the air that harbors lightning, or a place where lightning has been. It was faraway as morning yet, but it was all around her, and when she thought of turning back it came drifting up the road behind her, so faint that she kept hoping she might be mistaken, and so menacing that she found herself quickening her pace, almost running, to keep ahead of it.

What is it, what is it? I know this smell. I know this fear. Nothing was moving on the road now but herself and whatever beast she smelled, not a bird, not the tiniest insect. The scent never grew any stronger, although she walked on for a long time, but gradually a dull red light began to appear far along the road ahead of her, and it was not dawn. There was a green glow under the red, a pale, icy green which made her think of some strange fire, but the light cast no shadow, nor did it make the road any brighter or warmer to travel. The unicorn's ears flattened back, and her white tail shivered against her sides as though a storm were upon her, but the oldest part of her, the part that was never afraid, thought calmly, I hope the butterfly found a warm place to sleep. This is no night for a lost butterfly.

Then she came around a bend in the road and saw the creature that squatted by the roadside. Its back was to her, but she saw that it had a human shape, and she knew that it was not human. It was hunched over a dark, shapeless bag, and whatever was in the bag glowed red and pale green and yet gave no light.

No animal in all the world could have heard the sound of the unicorn's breath, but the creature turned suddenly and saw her. Its face was almost a human face. "Welcome," it said. "Well met, my lady." Its voice was deep and hoarse, but not unpleasant. In mocking courtesy, it swept off the huge black hat it wore and bowed its body before her, and the stifled moonlight fell on shaggy, curling hair and on the two small horns that might almost have been curls themselves, but for the way they glimmered in the moonlight.

III

"My name is Azazel," the demon said. "What a pleasant surprise." The unicorn stood quite still and did not answer.

The demon's features were human, but his pale face was as triangular as a cat's. The pebbly skin was stretched tight over knobbly cheekbones, which seemed to support the rest of his face, and his chin was deeply cleft. He had thin lips, red and waxy as chokecherries, and his smile seemed to flicker over his face like torchlight. His low forehead swooped down over huge eyesockets where his eyes shone yellow and lidless. The unicorn could see nothing of his body, for he was swathed from neck to foot in a black cloak. Where the hood fell back on his shoulders, a great hump stood up, bowing his body, looming higher than his head, heavy as fear made flesh. "This is a surprise," he said again. "I thought all you people were gone long ago. Dead as unicorns, as we used to say." He parted his lips slightly, and the unicorn saw long teeth gleam distantly, like fish turning in deep water.

The smell of lightning filled the unicorn's body. She said, "I know you. A thousand years ago, you came hunting a knight through my forest. I hid behind a tree, because I was a colt then, and my horn was like a blade of grass, but I remember how you hunted him up and down my forest with three red dogs and a red hawk. His horse screamed, and so did he, and so did I, but you never made a sound. The grass has never grown back where the dogs pulled him down." She was trembling, and she had to speak very slowly.

"Not I," said Azazel politely. "When you were a colt, I was already in the policy-making division. No doubt you have me confused with some rank-and-file demon. Anyway," he added with a touch of wryness, "we don't do that sort of thing anymore. Oh, it looked showy, and it was all right for the legends and the ballads—awful songs, inaccurate,

downright lies, really—but it was terribly inefficient. We do much better than that now. If I could
show you—" He fumbled vaguely in the inner
pockets of his cloak. "If I had my pamphlets here,"
he muttered. "They didn't even give me time to take
my pamphlets. I had a complete set."

For a moment it seemed to the unicorn that the
hump between his shoulders shifted sluggishly and
changed its shape. But it did not move again, and
she looked into the demon's yellow, guttering eyes,
and asked, "Why are you on this road, then? What
do you hunt now?"

Accidentally, she stirred the battered bag of fire
with a forefoot, and the demon snatched it away
from her and hugged it into his cloak. "It's a public
road," he snapped back at her. "I can be on it if I
want to. And I might ask you the same question.
What may a unicorn be doing on a superhighway?"

"I seek my people." That time she would have
sworn the hump moved, softly, lurchingly, as a cliff
crumbles.

"And I flee mine." Azazel laughed bitterly. His
voice became harsh, and yet almost singing. "Consider well what you see, white lady. I, Azazel, once
one of the Nine Commanders, and junior only to

Asmodeus and Astaroth; Master of the Hounds of
the Chasse Gayere; possessor of no one below the
rank of bishop; Judge of the Middle Court; and
First Lutanist at the pleasure of my shining lord—I
sit here now, on a strange road in a strange night,
exiled from my home as punishment for a crime
against Hell itself, a betrayer of betrayers, a sinner
against sin. Behold, I am monstrous in mine own
eyes, and I will not show myself. And I haven't
even got my pamphlets," he added forlornly. "Fan-
tastic artwork, and the whole format—" He broke
off, and his voice rumbled out like chariot wheels
once again. "Ask me no more. I pray you, ask me
no more."

The hump on his back made a sound between a
snort and a honk, and said, "Let me out of here, I
have to throw up." It moved grumblingly under the
black cloak like a great egg, ready to hatch. "Let me
out of here," it said. "That did it, boy. That last bit
did it. That was too much to bear."

"Be quiet," Azazel said sharply. He slapped
blindly between his shoulders at it, but the hump
was wriggling frantically now, and the blows
glanced off. "That's all, boy," it grunted. "Let me out
of this gunny sack, you big phony, you cockalovitch

drum major, you. Oh boy, this got to stop." It flailed around wildly on Azazel's back, muttering to itself, and the black cloak billowed and flapped despite the demon's desperate efforts to hold it in place.

As the unicorn stared, too astonished to be afraid anymore, the cloak split open along a seam and a second head popped into view, thrashing like a branch in the wind at the end of a long, boneless neck. It was a small head, somehow goatlike in its shape and in the curve of its puny horns, and even in the patchy tuft of beard on its chin. Its skin was wrinkled and crackly as a dead leaf, and its green eyes glinted more malevolently than Azazel's teeth. Grotesquely graceful, the neck arched out at a wide angle so that the head could look directly at Azazel. "One of the Nine Commanders," it mimicked the demon in a shrill, almost-musical voice, like a pitch-pipe full of sand. "Judge of the Middle Court, big shot of the Chasse Gayere. Hooboy, I have stood enough of this. Vice-president in charge of copyright, that's what *you* were, boy. Assistant secretary of the Chamber of Commerce, and only because nobody else could take shorthand. Feh, you hear me? Even Dante wouldn't have anything to do with you, the way you ran after him to put

45

you in his stupid book. Everybody else he put in, but not you. Some gangster you were, boy. Feh."

Azazel was actually blushing; his pale face had gone maroon with embarrassment. "That's enough," he mumbled, unable to look at the unicorn. "She isn't interested in all that."

The second head seemed to notice the unicorn for the first time. It stared at her in frank appraisal, then grinned with stubby teeth and said, "Hey. Hey, I didn't know they were making your kind these days. Boy, I could see why the old Sahib was carrying on like how art thou fallen from heaven." It turned back to Azazel and went on, "A little out of your class, though, old captain, a little out of your price range. Possessor of bishops!" Azazel closed his eyes. "They wouldn't even trust you with a Baptist faith healer. Bwana, it's a good thing you don't make you as sick as you make me, because we would be one miserable demon together." It coiled itself on Azazel's shoulder and winked at the unicorn.

"Ignore him," Azazel said wearily. "He shows off for strangers. All strangers."

"But who is he?" the unicorn asked, blinking dazedly from one head to the other. "And who are you, and what are you both? And how many demons are you, anyway?"

"We are me," Azazel answered. "I mean, we are Azazel, both of us. But the name is mine." Trying to patch together his air of menacing dignity, he insisted, "Don't forget that. I'm the one you read about. You call me Azazel. He has no name."

"Have so," the second head retorted. "One thing I've got, it's a name, boy. I've got a beauty."

Azazel turned on him so that both their heads, the shaggy and the scrawny, were in profile to the unicorn. "You can't keep telling people that's your name," he protested angrily. "It's not your name, it was never inscribed in the Book, you just took it for yourself. It's a stupid name for a demon, anyway. No more majesty than a hiccup."

"And Azazel's better." The head snickered wickedly. "Azazel. Hoo. Sounds like a sneeze in a bathtub."

Oh, a world, a world indeed, the unicorn thought. The people go blind, and the dragons weep, and the butterflies are mad, and the demons sit by the road and quarrel like puppets. Hoping to quiet them, she asked the second head, "What is your name? I have none."

The head gave her a look that might have been one of gratitude if he had not been a demon. "Webster," he answered. "That's my name now. *Webster.*" He savored the syllables, speaking them with a cold, innocent sweetness. "Boy, what a sound," he murmured. "Web. Ster. Webster. That's my name."

"Webster," Azazel sneered. "There's a name to rattle castles, there's a name to frighten children, there's a name for incantations." He burlesqued a witch's snarling shrillness. "O great Webster, powerful though scrawny; O most potent and maleficent Webster with the bad breath; O Neck, O Adam's-Apple, O Wondrous Beard; O Webster, Webster, Lord Omnipotent and also scabbed, appear, Webster, appear, appear!" He chortled contemptuously. "You always did have a sense of tradition," he said. "The only demon in Hell who knew how things ought to be done. Pitchforks and boiling oil, and the air full of volcanic ash all the time, because that's the way it's always been done. We have a reputation to maintain. Thousands of clergymen depending on us. Can't let the boys down, can we, in their hour of crisis? People who don't believe in Hell can't go there, can they? So everybody up, up, up, let's all get dressed up in our red demon suits again. Those terrible, smelly, red suits. One look at them and it's a three-day rash for sure. And *hot?*" Almost appealingly, he turned to the unicorn. "Now you show me where it says in the Bible that demons are all crazy mad for heat. We're damned too, remember. Some of us like to make things a little easier for ourselves, a little more civilized. You understand, I'm sure."

"Shoo," Webster cackled. "Some of us don't even call them *the damned* any more, we say *our unfortunate clientele.* Some of us were all going to have our horns crew-cut, that's how civilized we were."

Azazel flushed guiltily again, but he stroked his own darkly shining horns with an air of complacency. "Nobody clipped my horns," he said. "We were just talking about it, but I never would have let them do it."

"Mostly because we got thrown out too soon. You got a pretty civilized set of hands on you, though. Show the lady, why don't you? Probably impress her to pieces."

The demon put his hands behind his back, but not before the unicorn had noticed that the lean fingers ended in the stumps of heavy, hawklike talons, trimmed raggedly across. "You got thrown out," he retorted. "Remember that. You got thrown out, not me. I can go back and welcome anytime I want to, once I figure out a way to unhook you from the back of my neck. And I'm working on it, little friend. I'm working on it all the time."

"You'd keep tipping over," Webster warned him amiably. "Also, you'd have to fight your dandruff all by yourself. Also you'd be lonely. It's been a long time."

"A blowtorch," Azazel mused. "That's what I need, one of those." He looked hopefully at the unicorn, but she did not speak. A cold dawn breeze touched her, and she shuddered once, quickly, as though she had just wakened out of a long dream. For a moment, she could not remember a single detail of her long journey, and she asked herself dazedly, what place is this, how did I come here? Why am I here and not home? How old am I? She shook her head, trying to rid herself of the feeling of being in two times at once, and said to Azazel, "I never heard of a demon being thrown out of Hell before."

"Never will again," Webster answered proudly. "I'm the only trouble maker they ever had. Reactionary influence was how they said it." He chuckled happily. "That's a good name too. I almost took that one instead of Webster."

"The Council voted on it," Azazel explained. "We always vote now. Expulsion requires a two-thirds majority. They got it." He sighed. "I understood perfectly. I was with them in principle, but I did think they could have deliberated a bit more, considering whom the little rat was attached to. I would have liked them not to be quite so eager about it."

"But what did they expel you for?" the unicorn asked.

"Sedition and sabotage," Azazel replied.

"Messing around," Webster answered. "Just messing around."

The air was growing lighter and thinner, and as the shadows drew back from Azazel, his face began to seem less saturnine, and almost despairing. His hair was not as thick as the unicorn had imagined. "The speeches weren't so bad," he said. "We're a fairly tolerant community these days, and anyone can say pretty much whatever he likes, within reason. We're rather proud of that aspect, as a matter of fact. And besides, nobody ever blamed me for anything Webster said. They were very fair about the whole thing."

"One imp used to throw rocks at me all the time," Webster interrupted. "Only encouraging thing that's happened in a hundred years. That was a good kid."

"But the fires were what did it," Azazel went on. "Liberalism's all very well, but once he started setting fire to things, something had to be done. Belphegor put it very well, I thought. He said, 'Liberty is not license.' I've always believed that. Almost always," he added, as Webster giggled raspingly.

"I don't understand," the unicorn said. "I used to think of Hell as a great meadow of fire and a cold wind shaking the flames like grass. Isn't it like that?"

Webster's giggle became a hoot of delight. Azazel coughed, looked quickly from the unicorn's eyes to her feet, and said, "Well. No, not exactly. That is, the fires are all out. We put them out. We felt it gave people a bad impression, damaged the image somewhat. No, we're against fire. It's part of our policy now."

"Oh," said the unicorn. Webster began to sing quietly to himself in a happy voice. There was no tune to the song, and the unicorn could hardly make out the words, but they went something like this:

> Oh, I got the shopping center,
> and the pretty plastic houses,
> and I also got the television sta-tion
> and the bank went up,
> and the golf course went,
> and the subways are with us no more,
> and I got fourteen office buildings
> and a laun-dro-mat.

"Also, I singed the hell out of the parking meters," he added cheerfully. "Boy, they're hard to burn. I don't know anything that's harder to burn than a parking meter."

"He got hold of the body," Azazel explained. "My body. He can do that if I'm not on guard. I'm careful, don't you worry, but it just happens sometimes."

"In the middle of the night," Webster sang. "Tippy-toe, tippy-toe, *zwooosh*! The Scrawny Pyro strikes again! Supermarket goes up like a flower! Tippy-toe, tippy-toe, *zwooosh*! Hoo-*boy*!" He glared accusingly at Azazel. "Hadn't been for you taking over when you did, they'd never have got me. Old Grabs here."

"I knew my duty," Azazel said sternly. "Disturbed behavior is something we all understand and tolerate these days, but all these anti-social punks got to go. Belphegor said that."

"Boy, you had a better time at that trial than anybody," Webster muttered. He grinned at the unicorn and said, "And they threw us out. And here we are."

"Yes," Azazel's voice was suddenly soft. "Indeed. Here we are." He turned his head slowly back and forth, watching the coaches pass by, their roofs pink and silver in the early sunlight. "Amazing," he murmured. "Really amazing, when you think of it. I think there might be worse places for a demon to be exiled."

"Where will you go now?" the unicorn asked.

Azazel shrugged. "I don't know," he replied. "Everywhere. I'm looking for a special place."

"So am I," the unicorn said.

The demon let his hand fall on the little bag in his lap. "Look at that," he said. In the light of day, the cold fire still breathed and coiled as restlessly as ever. "Do you know what that is?" The unicorn did not answer.

"It's a coal from Hell." Azazel almost whispered the words, and even Webster glanced around nervously. "They put out all the fires, but I saved this and I hid it. If they knew, if they ever found out, they'd be after us like hornets." The touch of his former satanic bearing that had been cautiously reasserting itself collapsed completely. "I don't want it," he whimpered. "I wish I hadn't taken it. I don't know why I did. They'll tear us to pieces when they find out."

"Pull the fat self together, captain," Webster told him harshly. "You know what we're going to do with it. Find a good spot and start up our own Hell. Don't panic now." His eyes were glittering with anticipation; he spat yellow to sizzle on the road. "We'll fix those nogoods, boy. Wait'll we get our own Hell going. They can't stand competition, not that miserable community center. We'll mess with them proper. All we got to do is find the right spot."

"I don't know, I don't know." Azazel rocked to and fro, quaking in the sunlight. "They'll be after us, all of Hell out to get one coal back. They'll scatter us across the sky, like bloody clouds." His eyes widened with sudden hope. "I could tell them it was you. I could say you got control again and made me steal the coal. They'd believe me. They know I'm one of them."

"Save it," Webster answered. "They'll string us up together. Probably save rope and just wrap my neck around the branch a couple of times." His chuckle was almost pleasant. "I think that'd be nice. Neck to neck, from the same branch, a couple of dangling buddies. That's pretty."

Azazel stopped moaning long enough to say, "That's the most revolting image I've ever heard." Then he went back to moaning. Webster sighed and said, "Feh. And they'll find us, too. Some idea." He, too, was beginning to look worried; the goat head turned and turned on the long neck, straining to be free of it, the unicorn thought, like a kite in a storm.

She found herself feeling sorry for both of them, for Azazel who squatted disconsolately with his head in his clawless hands, smaller and older than he had appeared in the night; and Webster, trying as desperately to hold on to his own kind of bravado as Azazel had. They are demons, she told herself—*a* demon, I must remember that—and they have the lightning-smell about them, the smell of old evil, caked on them like sweat. They deserve whatever happens to them, I suppose. But they make such an inefficient demon, the two of them together. I can't imagine a Hell or a Heaven making much use of them, no more than this world can of me. We mean nothing to man or demon now. These two have outlived their own evil—and I my good? I don't know. I mustn't think of that.

"You may travel with me, if you care to," she said, reminding herself wryly that one should always speak most formally to demons. "My company is proof against all the wings of evil. Or it used to be," she added frankly. "The world is different, everything has changed so. I don't know if I have any power anymore. But you're welcome to come with me, if you choose."

Azazel's gape of astonishment narrowed gradually to a dubious frown, but Webster croaked, "Saved! The cavalry is arrived!" He arched his head out towards the unicorn, saying, "Right on the tip of the nose. Hold still, little flower." She stepped away in some alarm, and Webster swung his head back to Azazel. "Fats, that's it, who'd figure a demon to be running around with a unicorn? They'll boil the ocean before they come near her. Oh, we are saved, boy. Saved is what we are." He rested his chin on top of Azazel's head and closed his eyes in rapture.

"I have to consider this," Azazel said slowly. "I appreciate your offer, you understand, but I have my own reputation to think about." On his head Webster gave a squawk of inarticulate rage and protest, but Azazel went on, "After all, we are trying to create a good public image, to attract a respectable class of customers. And what mortal would sell his soul to a demon he suspected of associating with unicorns? Webster, my little Doré-Bible buddy, you ought to think of things like that. They won't have any confidence in us, and the demon who can't inspire confidence might as well be human. Belphegor said that."

"Belphegor," Webster said. "Oh, yes. Public image. Customers. Confidence. Yes, indeed. Shoo. Effendi, bwana, sahib, what you have done is, you have misunderstood. I tell you right now—" but he broke off sharply as Azazel snapped, "Down!" The black cloak swirled once, and Webster vanished as if something had pulled him down into dark water. Azazel said, "Excuse me," to the unicorn, and squatted as low as he could, sidling to keep her between him and the road.

The unicorn turned her head and saw that one of the iron coaches was stopping a little way from them. She liked neither its smell nor the sound it made, but she stood still and watched, thinking, there must be some reason for things like this, even if they seemed ugly to me. I must learn. A man and a woman stepped out of the coach and came toward her.

They were both young. The man was tall and thin, and he wore his hair, his shirt, and his trousers very short. There was nothing in his face to displease the unicorn, or to keep her from forgetting it even as she looked at him. But the girl was another matter, for she smelled like a forest far more beautiful than the unicorn's own, a wood full of birds bright enough to blind; of strange, singing beasts; and of trees like waterfalls. This is the way that virgins smell, and unicorns, who dream of that forest whenever they sleep, serve and guard all virgins, and come when they call, and know when they marry.

And yet there was something wrong, and the unicorn knew it and tried not to know. Far back in her throat, the dear scent tasted like milk that is within a breath of turning sour, and there was a feeling of chalk in her mouth. Nevertheless, telling herself, *it must be me, how could I be mistaken?*, she lowered her head in token of submission to the girl and said, "Command me," as she had said it so many times, so long ago, to so many frightened girls carrying totally unnecessary golden bridles. I hope she understands me, she thought. Even in this world, a virgin must surely be able to hear me.

A hand touched her face lightly, and instantly drew away. The man said, "Go on, it's all right. Don't be scared."

"They bite," the girl's voice said. "My brother got bitten by a horse once."

THE LAST UNICORN: THE LOST JOURNEY

"Nah, it's okay, he's tame." The unicorn felt a thick hand pat her neck and tug at her mane, in a kind of parody of the way the little boy had stroked her. Outraged, she jerked her head away, keeping it low so that her horn pointed at the man's body. "Don't touch me," she said. "She may touch me, but not you. You have no right." The feeling of wrongness, of nightmare mockery, was growing stronger in her. The smell, she thought. It's real, but it's not what I mean, not what I remember.

"Herbie, watch out." The girl giggled nervously. "He'll bite your hand off."

"Animals like me," the man reassured her. "I don't know why it is. Come here, boy, come on, got something nice for you." He made a sound with his mouth like bugs plopping into a pool.

"Don't touch me again," the unicorn warned him, but the girl only laughed as if she were very cold, and the young man came on, reaching out his cupped hand with nothing in it. The unicorn braced her hind legs for the charge and wondered if she would truly be able to go through with it. "Please don't touch me," she said.

Then the girl made a soft little scream, and the unicorn turned to see Azazel standing up behind her. His legs were very bowed, as if the weight of the seeming hump on his back had spraddled them, and he moved like a dancing bear in the circus. But he smiled sweetly as he came towards the young man and the girl. "How do you do?" he said. "My name is Azazel."

The girl moved close to the man's side, and he put his arm around her without looking at her. Azazel's smile widened, curving like the wings of a distant bird. "My name is Azazel," he said again. The great hump shifted a trifle, as though Webster were thinking of making an entrance, but it did not move again.

"Herbie, be careful," the girl whispered loudly in the man's ear. "He looks like some kind of a beatnik.

"Nah. Where's his beard? He's just got a hump." Aloud, he said to Azazel, "Hey, we just stopped to look at the horse. Didn't know he belonged to anybody."

Azazel's face had fallen perceptibly as he heard their whispering, but he answered calmly, "She does not belong to me. Only people belong to Azazel. That's my name, Azazel."

"Herbie, I don't care what you say, he *is* a beatnik!" The girl's hand dived into her purse and came out with a tiny metal box. She held it up against her face, and the sun glinted off it, making the unicorn blink. There was a soft click, and the girl lowered the box, smiling at nothing. Like a lover, the unicorn thought.

"Well," the young man said. "Well, we just wondered. You a painter or something?"

Azazel shook his head. "No. No, I'm not a painter. I'm a demon. Azazel, you know. One of the Nine Commanders."

The girl clicked the box again as the couple were retreating to their coach, which was not at all an easy thing to do, as she was backing up and being dragged at the same time. Azazel called his name after them hopefully, but they jumped into the coach and it was off with a sound like surf. The demon's face wrinkled in fury, and the air was savage with the smell of lightning. His hands moved above his head like smoke, and he made a gesture as if he were hurling something after the coach. But it reached a bend in the road and vanished, unharmed.

After awhile, Azazel sighed and said, "Imagine that. Now that's never happened to me before."

"No. Never." The unicorn felt very tired.

"I see a few difficulties here," Azazel said. "Well, it's an open field, and publicity does wonders. We might have to buy television time." He turned to the unicorn. "If I may still accept your offer? I have a feeling we'll both need company." The unicorn nodded without speaking. The virgin-scent was rancid in her throat, and her heart ached with confusion and loss.

They set off down the black road, the unicorn walking slowly to match Azazel's bandy-legged pace. He was irritatingly cheerful and chatty at first, although the unicorn hardly ever answered him. I've done so much talking since I left my forest, she thought, more than I've done in hundreds of years. I don't want to talk anymore.

"I wouldn't have cared for them as clients anyway," Azazel was saying. "Especially the woman. She looked like an orange. What terrible prospects these people are. Imagine not recognizing a demon in broad daylight. Low-class types. They'd have to pay me to haul their souls away."

The unicorn did not answer, and they walked on in silence until they came to the bend in the road. The coach was stopped a few hundred feet in front of them, all four of its wheels torn and misshapen.

The young man was standing in the middle of the road with his coat off, looking at the coach, but not doing anything. When he saw them coming he went and sat inside the coach with the girl, and they sat very still watching the unicorn and the demon walk by. The unicorn remembered for a long time how the two sand-colored faces peered from behind the glass.

"A spiteful magic," she said to Azazel, trying not to be amused. "It did you no good."

"That's what you think," Webster's voice rasped in her ears. "He was trying for an earthquake."

Azazel smiled painfully. "Demons have little power in this new world, it seems."

"Unicorns have none," she said.

"Really?" Azazel sounded politely relieved. "Oh, what a pity. Well, you can buy television time, too. That's one of the nicest things about this age," he added thoughtfully. "We don't really need the old powers, after all. You'll see."

IV

A blue jay swooped low over them on that first day of their journey, said, "Well, I'll be a squab under glass," and flapped straight home to tell his wife about it. She was sitting on the nest, quietly cursing their four eggs. "*Hatch*, you little devils," she kept muttering, "*Hatch*, you nasty, wretched, life-wrecking monsters! Hatch, and let's get it over with, you horrid, ugly, featherless. . . . Why can't I have kittens, just once, or rabbits, just for something soft to sit on? *Hatch*, damn it!"

"Saw a unicorn today," the blue jay said as he alighted.

"Isn't that nice," his wife replied coldly. "Was that before or after you and the boys saw the pink elephants?"

"Baby, a unicorn!" The jay abandoned his casual air and hopped up and down on the branch. "I haven't seen one of those since the time—"

"You've never seen one," she said. "This is me, remember? There isn't a story of yours I don't know."

The jay paid no attention. "There was a hunch-backed party in black with her," he rattled. "Bound over Cat Mountain, they were, couldn't tell you why—nothing but scrub and thorn on the other side. Absolutely fascinating, I couldn't take my eyes off them."

"For three hours?" His wife's tone was danger-ously quiet.

"Well, I might have followed them just a little way," the jay admitted. "I can't help it, I've always been inquisitive, you know that. Constantly probing, questioning, taking nothing for granted, that's me. And then some of the boys happened along, and they got curious too—"

"I told you what would happen if I ever caught you hanging around with those people again," his wife said. She advanced on him, her neck feathers ruffling.

"Honey, we weren't—I didn't—" the jay began, and she knew he hadn't, but she batted him one anyway. Blue jays' wives get very tired of blue jays sometimes.

But the unicorn and the demon waked on through the world, keeping well to the side of the road, and not one person who passed them by knew them for what they were. Very often, the coaches would sound their horns at them like savage iron geese, sometimes to warn Azazel to get his horse off the road, but more often simply to see them jump. The unicorn got over her fear of the noise in time, but she always became curiously, lingeringly sad at the sight of a coach window jammed with red, squalling faces, their mouths staring open as if the horn-sound were coming from somewhere inside them, their hands waving up and down like sea-anemones. Azazel ignored them, but the unicorn would gaze far down the road long after they were gone, until the next load of mouths and hands came by, yelping and laughing, and, she sometimes thought, dully frightened.

Don't care, she commanded herself. You have no reason to care about them, and no right to wish they were as you remember them. You never

PETER S. BEAGLE

noticed them unless they did you honor; don't complain now that they forget you. But the clear, lonely smell of the virginity she served wandered back to her from so many of the flying coaches that she was never able to escape the feeling of need all around her, and though each breath she drew left its tiny sourness in her mouth, still she turned this way and that to find it, still she told herself, this is the way purity smells nowadays. I must get used to it. And, over and over, *it must be me, it is surely my fault, somehow.*

Traveling with any companion at all, even another unicorn, would have been strange and unsettling for a creature as solitary-minded as herself, but the wanderer at her side was a demon, and the very smell of him would have her feet skittering as awkwardly as a colt's to be away, lest his shadow touch her. And yet, it was not fear she felt for Azazel; nor liking, for that matter; nor pity. She did not know the word, for she had few names for anything anymore, but now and then, when they passed something that seemed beautiful or ugly to her—a valley embroidered with slender, violet trees, or a sudden bareness of houses, as alike as grains of sand, as arid as a desert—she found herself wondering what the demon saw there, and what he thought. And though she never asked, still this was a new thing for her, after a thousand years of life; for she was wise enough to know that she had never once been interested in the thoughts of any other being in all the world.

They went slowly in the first days of their acquaintanceship, following the black road high among mountains, and they spoke only seldom to one another. Once, when the steepness had slowed Azazel's odd, limping skip to a shuffle, he said, "I am very tired. Let me ride on your back for a little while, until I get my breath again."

No request could have terrified or offended her more. She imagined herself running with the demon steeds she had seen long ago, with a demon's chuckle in her head, and a demon's burning weight on her back, and her mane and tail aflame. The muscles of her body began to shiver and twitch, like little waves when a distant wind plucks at them, and she stared at the steps of her own shadow on the road to keep herself from bolting. Her voice was very calm and proud as she said, "None but virgins have ever ridden me, and none ever will."

Webster was muffled under Azazel's cloak, like

a pet bird at night, or a phrase like that would—she knew already—have brought him up with a howl of scorn and aggravation. But Azazel said only, "Ah, yes, virgins, yes, of course," sounding as if he were thinking of something else. They walked on without speaking for a long time before he added, almost apologetically, "Of course, if you wanted to raise a foolish technical question, you could point out that, in the actual physical sense, we're all virgins, we demons, every one of us. Accounts for a lot of our frustrations. Except the incubi and succubi, and they have their own frustrations. I only mention it for argument's sake, naturally."

"It was human virgins I meant," said the unicorn, beginning to feel uncomfortable in a different way.

Azazel's voice was as soft and cold as evening mist. "Yes, I'm sure. A human child, untouched. It is children we're talking about, isn't it? I mean, there is some sort of time limit on the legend?"

"I don't understand," she said. "Just virgins. I always liked to be near them, even when they had no need of me, when there was no danger to preserve them from."

"*Preserve* is a good word," Azazel murmured. "Did you ever wonder what happened to them after you got through preserving them? Did you ever wonder whose responsibility all those preserved virgins are?" The unicorn said nothing. "Well, you'll see. It's about time you good folk found out what kind of material we've had to work with lately. Keep them pure, by all means, swoop them away to safety on your back, but don't blame us when they turn out totally useless for good or for evil. It's not our fault. We do the best we can."

Most words spoken to her were like smoke to the unicorn, passing over her, turning color in the glow of her horn, but never touching her; too fragile to sound even the smallest bell in her heart. But Azazel's words seemed to walk heavily back and forth inside her, hurting her, and she did not know why. She said slowly, "Truly, I've never liked anyone to ride me, even the virgins. I think living in a house must feel like that, something always gripping your breath, no matter how gently. I would rather they never wanted to ride me at all. But they always do, and I let them."

"The backside of purity," the demon jeered. "That's what makes the martyrs." But the unicorn shook her head.

"No," she said. "I was never one of the good folk.

73

They are very good, I'm certain, but they always do so many things they don't want to do, and my people are not like that. I never minded the virgins. I loved the smell of them, and I loved their lightness. Sometimes, in my forest, squirrels drop down the trees onto my neck, or crickets run across my back when I lie down, and their lightness is like that. Their hearts are new, you see, and they have no sorrow."

"Their hearts are as rotted as mine," said Azazel, "and by the same little sorrows. Walk slower, then, since you won't carry me. I've got a bad leg."

After that time, he rarely spoke to her unless she spoke first, but his lips moved constantly as he recited the names of great evildoers to himself, taking comfort in their crimes. "It soothes me," he told her. "It's the only way I ever get to sleep, these nights." In addition, he was forever engaged in a running battle with Webster; they bickered constantly and violently in a language full of private meanings, each blaming the other for thousands of years' worth of misfortunes, persecutions, and lost opportunities. At first, all the clattering of their eternal war alarmed and angered the unicorn, from Azazel's wistfully elaborate threats,

THE LAST UNICORN: THE LOST JOURNEY

delivered in a tired, menacing monotone, to Webster's obscene pipe of defiance. But after awhile the weary go-round of it lulled her; they had nagged deep ruts into each other long before she was born; they were too worn into their roles now to pay the smallest attention to one another or to themselves, except now and then—and they made these occasions of awareness as brief as possible, scrambling for shelter under their grim banter like lizards in the hot sun. "We're damned too, remember," Azazel had said.

The fact of their exile gleamed bright and bitter in their long lives as a fresh blaze on an old tree. Azazel reviewed their trial ceaselessly, pacing in the cage of the verdict, going over the court procedure not with an eye to reversing the decision—he was completely in favor of it—but because he saw no real reason not to be on the winning side, instead of on Webster's. "I hate that righteous feeling," he said.

Webster, on the other hand, was happiest reliving the moment of his appearance on the witness stand; he had been his own defense attorney, as much through delight as necessity. "I was great," he said to the unicorn. "There I was, riding to my rescue,

wait, wait, nobody despair, I'm coming to save me.
I got up like this—" his long neck went suddenly
rigid as a gallows, so that his head stood high above
Azazel's—"and I went, '*J'accuse! J'accuse*, boy! My
friendless but lovable client is being railroaded all
to pieces, hey, and also framed, and it's just a dirty
shame, is what it is. Now I ask you, devils and
witches, I put it before you, imps, familiars, and
poltergeists, does this demon have the face of an
arsonist?'"

Azazel grunted sourly. "That sank it right there."

"I couldn't deny it." Webster sighed. "Mirrors
don't reflect us. I never knew what I looked like till
I got a look in a puddle a couple days ago. Boy, if
there's one kind of face I've got, that's it. How come
you never told me?"

"You'd have said I was lying."

"You would have been," Webster answered
cheerfully. "Anyway, on the way out I got in a good
one. I said, okay, dear friends, okay, dear fellow-
passengers. Run the place just the way you want to,
boy. Modernize, clean up a little, get some of the
smoke out of the joint. No more brimstone lakes—
terrible smell, terrible—and let's do something
about those lava beds out there, they ruin the

tennis balls. Get rid of all the mountains of thorns and all the flame trees, or the people won't be able to see the billboards. And the monsters got to go, all of them, they lower property values. No, wait a minute, may as well keep the monsters. They might come in handy for rush hours and stuff. And maybe psychiatrists, the ones that know how to smile. What do those things with the claws do, those harpies? They fly around and torment people? Run them off, we don't need them, we've got all the cops. Think big, good buddies, think modern, think like people. People know how to run a hell, you can't go wrong with people." The goat head giggled rustily and rested its chin between Azazel's horns; an uncomfortable position, but Webster's favorite traveling spot because Azazel hated it.

"But nobody's ever going to write poems about you anymore, boy," he said, almost to himself. "You've had all your poems. And no one'll ever be really afraid of you again."

"Get off," Azazel said wearily. He swatted at Webster, who cringed out of range, cackling with ancient triumph. "Nobody wants poems," Azazel said, "not on earth and certainly not in Hell. People don't believe in poems, and we can't do anything with things people don't believe in. As for being afraid—" He looked sideways at the unicorn and a corner of his mouth stretched slowly upwards, like a snake. "What good is their fear to us? Let them rather fear each other, as they do every minute they live, let them fear the world they make. They've never feared Hell as they fear their own lives." His smile grew wider, almost kindly except for the sharp shine of his teeth. "Besides," he said, "if they were afraid of us, they wouldn't come to stay with us after they die. We have to make them think of Hell not as the Pit, not as the Furnace, but as their eternal home."

"Shoo," Webster said. "That's it right there. Not Hell, but home. No demons, just your friends and neighbors. No fire, just your very own home town, we've kept it just the way it was when you left it, ain't changed a thing. And no furies, no harpies, no torturers—man, *no*—just you and your loved ones. We got a lot of love down here. Sit down, take a load off your feet, rest you merry. Welcome home."

"How well you put it." Azazel saw a cigarette butt lying in the road, and snatched it from under the unicorn's feet a second before Webster's head and neck swooped down with a hiss and whistle to clash its teeth on pebbles. Azazel chuckled delightedly and gnawed the cigarette butt like a carrot. Cigarettes were all either of them ever ate on earth, and they fought over each one in murderous silence. Azazel said, "Face it, colleague. The Hell you want back woke up one morning from a restful dream of the Dark Ages, and realized that when it came to weaving really artistic anguish of soul, it was a long way behind the lives of men. And do you know what happened to your clanking, medieval Hell, dear old friend? It died of sheer embarrassment. And the infant Hell that took its place is going to have to grow like mad before it can offer man pain to equal even the small, mean sufferings they take so much for granted as their own faces. The time of great punishments is long gone, gone with the great sinners. This is an age of pinpricks, constant little bloodlettings that never have time to heal. And the Hell must suit the age, always."

He made a sudden grab at Webster, still resting between his horns, and barely missed him. The little demon was silent for awhile, and then said sullenly, "Well, not in my Hell, boy, none of that at Webster's place. There's people over here, and there's demons over there, and one thing about my

Hell, you'll always be able to tell the people from the demons."

"Precisely," Azazel answered. "And there's your mistake, and Satan's great folly as well."

"Excuse me," the unicorn said. She had not meant to pay attention to them, but for once the rhythm of their two voices scratched at her mind instead of soothing it. She said, "You spoke of having to entice people to Hell of their own wills. I was always told they were sent there, or to Heaven, this way or that way, no matter what they wanted. I thought it was judgment."

It was the first time she had ever heard Azazel and Webster laugh together, and the sound of it made her think of the coal Azazel carried in his bag, the flame that gave no more warmth than a star. The two heads looked at one another when they stopped laughing, and Azazel said in a friendly tone, "You tell her. You ought to be the one."

"It ain't like that anymore, little flower," Webster explained. "Nobody judges nobody, nobody makes nobody go anywhere he doesn't think he wants to. You do it all yourself, nobody cares. You pick the place you think you might be happy, and you're always wrong, every time. That's the best part of it, for a demon. I got to admit it wasn't near as much fun the other way."

"You're thinking of Satan's time," Azazel said to her. "But Satan doesn't have very much to do with management anymore. He began losing interest some time ago—about the time the telephone was invented, I should say—and he's really practically retired now. Beelzebub runs things these days, Beelzebub and an enterprising chap named Rosier. He invented love. Oh, Satan still has all his titles, and you have to get his signature on so many papers, and when he comes to board meetings everybody has to be kind to him and make him feel useful. They ask his opinion on everything, of course, but he sits in his old chair and grunts, 'What the hell, who gives a damn? What the hell, who gives a damn?' That's all he ever says. We try to keep him out of the public eye as much as we can, for his own sake."

"Poor old guy," Webster muttered. "He's cold all the time since they put the fires out, don't matter how many blankets you give him. There's this other old cat comes around sometimes to keep him company, and they visit back and forth a lot. Funny thing to see, the two of them sitting around in their blankets, just looking at each other. Sometimes they pay chess or something, but most of the time they just sit there."

"The other one," the unicorn said. "Is he God?" The names of God and the Devil meant very little to her, but she always thought of them together, as if they were married.

Azazel shrugged. "I have no idea. Somebody is." He turned his head quickly to look over his crooked shoulder at the road behind them. He did that often, although there was never anything following them but shadows and machines. The little sack of fire brushed the unicorn's side, and she shivered and moved away. Azazel said, "I wonder who's master *there* now. I wonder what they're offering."

He stared at her out of the yellow eyes that were not really firelike by day but the color of faded leaves. "And I wonder about you," he said, "and the creatures like you, the half-beasts, the creations. Whose are you, where do you belong, the unicorns, the dragons, the centaurs, the griffins, the mermaids, the sea serpents? Heaven and Hell fight and sleep, paint their faces, and fight and sleep, but what happens to you? You were here before we were, but where will you go? Why do you never change? You can't live without changing, not any more." His limping feet clicked along the black road, light feet, goat feet.

"Creatures like me?" she said. "There are no other creatures like me."

Azazel made a scraping sound in his throat, and a few wildflowers by the roadside turned brown and brittle. Webster giggled hoarsely. "That's gone too, dad. From now on we got to pick them, just like people." Azazel did not answer.

One morning, before dawn, they passed through a small village where no one was awake. The unicorn feared cities without knowing why, and walked around them when they barred her way, much to Azazel's displeasure. But she liked to look at the houses in the dusty blue light. They were like shells, she thought; they even smelled a little of the sea. Scattered along both sides of the road, thin and separate, with no second row of houses behind them, they seemed very delicate, and she felt a kind of pity for them, as though the houses were her sleeping children. Wait until the light changes, she thought. I won't like them anymore when the sun comes up. I never do.

Then she heard a girl singing, and she turned to

see. The girl was coming across the road towards them, her head held a little low, and her hands binding back her hair, and she was singing in a clear, quiet voice.

> *What is plucked will grow again,*
> *What is slain lives on,*
> *What is given will remain,*
> *What is gone is gone.*

She was not a pretty girl, but she had a rare gracefulness about her, and she seemed pleased to be alive and moving. Humans used to look like that, the unicorn thought. Or is it only that I choose to remember them so?

At the first sound of the girl's voice, a remarkable change had come over Azazel and Webster. The little demon huddled into the cloak and lay perfectly still, while Azazel hunched his body even more than usual and adopted a ludicrous waddle, almost like squatting, with his arms dangling lifelessly at his sides and his eyes fixed on his own feet. The unicorn looked down at him and said interestedly, "You remind me of a dwarf I saw once, a long time ago. He was a king's trainbearer, the poor little thing, and I remember how the others—"

"Be still!" the demon hissed at her. She thought she heard Webster snicker. Then the girl was saying pleasantly, "Good morning to you, stranger. Are you going far?"

"To the moonfall," Azazel answered her, "to the land's end and back again." He was using the throaty demon-voice he saved for special occasions, and the unicorn would have been amused if she had not sensed, underneath the richness, the rasping breath of a tired, trapped animal. He said, "I am only a humble but honest peddlerman, good lady, journeying through the towns in search of fortune, adventure, and a friendly death, satisfied with simple things, sleeping where I can, eating what kindness and a little trickery provide, content to take the world as it takes me, and singing now and then about it all." He caught his breath and added, "By cracky."

The girl smiled, showing very white teeth. "It's been a long time since a peddler passed this way," she said. "I didn't know there were any left. What do you sell?"

"Oh, Lor' bless you, mum," Azazel answered quickly, "I am laden with all sorts of gimcracks and gaudy gewgaws, fripperies, filigrees, and fooleries, not to mention frivolities, fancies, and fiddledee-dees. I have all kinds of iridescent idiocies, and any number of oddities, ordinary or obsolescent, as well as a fair supply of spangled sillinesses, though I may as well warn you, they're taking those off the market, and I won't be able to get you no spare parts nor replacements, ayup. I also carry, of course, a stock of the commoner baubles and jinglements, for those whose taste lies there. Also gum for the children, those as have them."

The girl was walking beside them now, peering over the unicorn's back at Azazel. He kept his head turned away from her and kept stumbling along in his ridiculous crouching gait. "How wonderful," she murmured. "And do you carry all those wares in a single satchel?" She pointed to the little bag dangling at the end of one of Azazel's limp arms, and she smiled again.

Azazel seemed to be trying to shrink out from under the lump that was Webster, and the effort made him look rather like a withered mushroom. "Samples," he croaked. "Tokens. Mere selections. Earnests, you might say. Symbols of the whole. Examples. A butter sandwich." He hugged the bag against himself with both hands.

Webster was now definitely making tiny, terrified sounds under Azazel's cloak; they sounded, to the unicorn's sharp ears, like a series of *yowps*, leavened with an occasional miserable *help*. But the girl did not seem to hear them. She laughed softly and asked, "Have you anything about you that I might use to light a fire? Matches, perhaps, or even a flint? I would pay you well."

The smell of the demons' fear burned so strongly in the unicorn's nostrils that she too began to be afraid, although she could feel no reason for it. The only strange thing about the girl walking at her side was that she seemed to have very little scent at all, of virginity or anything else. Her body held a distant odor of sweet smoke, and nothing more. But for the pleasantness of her voice and the ease of her moving, the unicorn would have paid little attention to her; yet terror of her was shaking Azazel to pieces, and not all the unicorn's senses and understandings could tell her why. Azazel was whispering, "No, no fire. None. Absolutely. No. No fire at all. No. Please."

"What a pity." The girl did not seem at all disappointed. She began to sing again.

> *What is seaborn dies on land,*
> *Soft is trod upon.*
> *What is stolen burns the hand,*
> *What is gone is gone.*

She patted the unicorn's nose with a small, cold hand. "A lovely animal," she said. "Well, then, do show me whatever you have in your bag. A woman likes to buy foolish things now and again."

In the shadow of his black hat, Azazel's face and

eyes had gone the yellow-white of stagnant water. "But I have nothing," he said. "A few trinkets, no more. I have nothing to show you."

"Then show me trinkets. See how shrewdly you have charmed me, peddler, and see how eager I am to buy. You won't find customers like me in the city. Open your bag, peddler."

"Pity an old man," Azazel whimpered, but the girl did not seem to hear him. The sun was beginning to rise, and Azazel turned suddenly towards her as though he had been counting on the dawn to dissolve her like mist. But she kept pace with him, smiling placidly. A few drops of water on her hair sparkled in the new sun. "Open your bag," she said.

Then Azazel sighed like a falling tree and straightened his body a little. He opened the bag cautiously, keeping it out of the girl's sight, although it seemed impossible to the unicorn to hide that coiling flame, cold and bright as the deepest of deep-sea fishes. He put his hand into the bag and held it there for a moment; his lips were moving and his face was as creased and as suddenly ancient as she remembered seeing it once before. When he took his hand out— slowly, very slowly, as though he were indeed tugging something up from the seabottom—the lean fingers were closed around a gold ring. He bowed and held it out to the girl. "From the Princess of Samarkand to you," he announced graciously. "The dear child is a compulsive crapshooter."

For the first time, the girl seemed a little disturbed. Her eyes flickered from the ring to Azazel and back, making the unicorn think of sharp-toothed little animals that moved like water. The girl said softly, "Show me some more," and Azazel groped in the bag again and brought up a necklace made of strange stones, the color of hunter's moons. "A caliph's gift," he explained to the girl. "He gave it to the wrong concubine and there was a bit of trouble at the time, but that's what it was made for." The girl fingered it impatiently. "More, peddler," she commanded. Her voice had grown a trifle shrill.

Azazel produced in succession a total of seven silver rings, six jeweled brooches, five assorted bangles, four blinding necklaces, three hammered bracelets, two diamond hatpins, and something that looked very much like a live bird before he stuffed it frantically back into the bag. Each effort seemed to cost him a gasp or a grunt of pain, as though he were giving birth to each bauble, and when at last he closed the bag and turned to face the girl fully, his face was livid and exhausted, his eyes empty of all but the faintest glitter of triumph. "Those are all the adornments I have left." His voice was terribly tired. "The cheaper ones, I may add."

The girl stood motionless, staring at Azazel, with her hands and arms and throat foaming and spilling over with gems and jewels; she might have been a statue of an influential goddess. The unicorn, who could scent fury as she could fear, could still smell nothing but the faint smokiness of the girl's body, and yet the stillness held a strange, bland menace that was somehow a shade darker than slithering rage and bared teeth. The girl stroked the unicorn again and said, "A lovely animal. A rare animal." She turned then and walked away, moving as sweetly as ever, back into the village where the unicorn could hear the first sounds of waking.

The unicorn would have watched her go, but Azazel was already scuttling away as fast as he could, without looking back to see if she followed. She caught up with him easily and asked. "Why are you running? Why were you so frightened of her? Who is she?"

Azazel slowed down long enough to dart her a glance in which spite, exhaustion, and real hatred were hopelessly confounded together. "'My company is proof against all the wings of evil,'" he mimicked her savagely. "How ducky. I can hardly wait till you learn to recognize evil, though you may very well be extinct by then." He tucked up his cloak and began running again, stumbling often, limping always, very much like a child who had just learned to walk the day before.

"I don't understand," the unicorn said helplessly. Azazel did not look at her again, but she heard him gasp out of the side of his mouth, "You never do. Part of your charm."

Puzzled and confused, she stopped short in the road, letting Azazel hobble along, and looked back towards the village. She could still see the girl, a tiny figure now, shining with Azazel's jewels, bright as snow. The unicorn had a moment to notice that the girl, like the demon, cast no shadow under the red sun—and then the girl was gone, glitter and all, vanished between one step and another as completely as a note of music. For an instant afterward, the smoky smell was very strong and sweet as death, so that the unicorn's body shuddered once as if all her bones had turned to sugar. After that, the scent was gone too, and

the unicorn could never quite remember it exactly
the way it had been.

V

Azazel did not stop running for a long time, not until the village was well out of sight and his pace had become no more than a heavy, struggling walk. The unicorn, trotting easily beside him, was almost moved to take him up on her back, but the fear of his cold skin was too great in her and she could not make herself speak. Webster finally slowed him down by popping his head out of the black cloak and saying crossly, "Captain, the novelty of this is wearing off something fierce, and it got to stop. You got me clanging around back here like unto a bag of roller skates."

Azazel came to a dead halt at last, but he did not turn to look back along the road. He stood very still for a while, with his eyes closed and his breath rattling like hail. "You forget how fast they are," he said. "It's easy to forget." He began to walk on again. "I miss the swiftness most," he complained quietly. "Humans move so slowly." His voice was gentle and dazed.

"I didn't know she was a demon," the unicorn said. Azazel did not seem to have heard her, but Webster answered, "Hard to tell with the new models, ain't it? Gets confusing for us sometimes."

But she said, "I should have known. I was made to know. I could always tell demons when I met them, and virgins, always, and I could smell sorrow and pain and madness, and kindness, now and then. Now everything smells the same to me, and I might as well be human for all I know, for all I can feel." Maybe I'm beginning to disappear, she thought. The dragon said I would.

Webster grinned, showing all his cindery teeth. "That's the idea, little flower. That's just the way it's supposed to be."

"So slowly," Azazel said in the same sleepy voice. "As if they were moving under water, and they never get anywhere anyway. Can't do better than that, can you? Can't even match it."

"Hey," Webster said worriedly. He hooked his long neck into a question mark to be able to look into Azazel's face. "Hey, you feel all right, glorious leader? Because you look like somebody pulled your plug out and you all sort of trickled away."

"I'm all right. I just didn't expect them to find out the coal was missing so soon. We haven't even tried to use it yet." He swayed suddenly, as if he had walked into the wind, but he did not fall. "I wonder if she recognized us. It's all over if she did."

"Nah," Webster said positively. "We were in disguise, don't forget."

"That's true. I thought I was pretty convincing. Charming and debonair, but touched with an old sadness. I convinced *me*." He turned to the unicorn and asked, "What did you think? How did I look?"

"Cramped," the unicorn said truthfully. "I didn't understand that part of it at all. Why were you crouching like that, and what was all that rainbow language for? What were you supposed to be?"

Azazel blinked at her. "Why, I changed my shape, of course. By a way of mine, I took on the seeming and semblance of a rascally old peddler—much traveled, wily but lovable, a shade wistful at times, but jaunty withal. An unforgettable character.

Wasn't I marvelous? You wouldn't have known me, would you? You'd never have known." There was a strange sound of pleading under his words.

"Azazel," the unicorn began. She had never spoken the demon's name before, and it seemed to be alive inside her mouth, biting and stinging. "Azazel, you didn't change your shape. You didn't look any different."

The two heads turned to stare at her. For a moment, they looked very much alike: the yellow eyes and the green eyes gone suddenly small and wary, like the eyes that move on stalks. Azazel suddenly opened his mouth wide, as if he were about to howl with frustration, and the shadow of his hat made it appear that he had lost all but a splintered few of his lion's teeth. But he closed his mouth and made no sound; instead, summoning all his haughtiness, he stood very straight and said, "We were in disguise. There never was a demon who lost the art of changing his shape."

The unicorn did not answer. Webster said sadly, "There is now, huh?"

"You might have forgotten the magic," she said, wanting to be helpful. "Why don't you try again and see if it works now?"

"One thing I hate, it's cheap sarcasm." Webster twined his neck almost lovingly around Azazel's. "Bwana, they have changed the combination on our old black magic, and we are about to get stomped flat. How about you kiss me once, before the end?"

Azazel unwound him counter-clockwise without even looking at him. "But we were in disguise," he insisted. "We were a lovable old peddler."

"You may well have been," Webster conceded. "But I have to admit, every time she looked at me I felt like I was wearing a big sign, and it said, *Some peddler, boy*, in red letters. That girl had a glance on her like the north wind." He shifted nervously on Azazel's shoulders, his long neck rippling as if the wind were still worrying it. "Was I us, comrade, I would start moving pretty fast. The whole gang of them's going to be after us before you could say help."

"I don't care," Azazel said quietly. He sat down by the roadside as gracefully and irrevocably as a falling leaf, crossing his legs and folding his hands. "I really don't care," he said, and he smiled at the unicorn. "Everybody thinks I care, but I don't. I am very old, and very far from home, and I haven't got enough magic left to fry an egg, and my feet hurt, and I'm just not going to get up anymore." He held the satchel in his lap and opened it for a moment to look at the coal. "It's dying, anyway," he said tonelessly. "The trees put it out." And to the unicorn's eye, the cold fire did seem to have grown a little duller and its strange breathing slower. It did not hurt her eyes to look at it now.

Webster stooped protectively over the satchel. "Well, sure it's dying, I know that. You can't carry one of those around forever, like a rabbit's foot. It's starving, it got to have things to eat." He stared accusingly at Azazel. "You going to just sit there and let it starve?"

Azazel appeared to be considering the matter carefully. "Yes, I think so. Of course, they may catch up with us first and take it away from us. It's hard to tell." He closed the bag and moved it out of Webster's reach. "I wish I could sleep," he said to the unicorn. "We can't, you know, none of us. I wish I could. I have so many ideas of what it must be like."

He yawned elaborately, and his body began to slump forward, making the unicorn think of a riverbank that the water had crumbled away. Looking at him, she could feel his tiredness eating at her own heart: the exhaustion of too much awareness, too long a life of lidless eyes; the weariness that never became sleep, but burned and burned coldly until, as with trees, the life silently gave way to stone, and there was nothing left of the soul but its immortality. Not I, she thought, not I, I'm alive, I'm not stone. Webster, still trying to coax Azazel to his feet, grinned savagely at her without speaking. *I am not like him*, she told herself desperately. *I am not like anyone.* And she wished, more than she had ever wished for anything, to be back in her forest, where she lived by herself, and never spoke to anyone, and did dancelike battle with old enemies who were very nearly old friends. I must go home, she told herself, while I still know what I am. And then, with Webster's grin still tweaking slyly at her, like monkey hands, she amended, before I know what I am.

"Where did the jewels come from?" she asked Azazel, "all the beautiful jewels you gave to the girl?" The demon made a swift flicking gesture with his hand, spreading the fingers as if he were pinching out a flame.

"I made them up," he said, "but that's not magic. That's knowing about reality, knowing how to use it. A baby could do it—some of them can. That's not real magic."

Webster seemed to be actually tugging at Azazel's tombstone body with his neck, vainly trying to haul him upright. The unicorn could imagine his head suddenly tearing away and sailing grandly off into the sun, spinning and swooping, the horned head to dream of the Pleiades, the neck to get caught in a tree. "Headmaster, sir, we got to get out of here," he was pleading; it was the first time the unicorn had ever seen him really alarmed. "You can't just sit here and wait for them."

"Bet me," said Azazel.

"But they will rend us limb from tree, old captain. There won't be enough of us left to count like lint. They're pretty bitter back there."

"Not at me. Nobody's mad at me." Azazel let the little demon whimper quietly for a moment before he added, "They won't hurt us. I don't think they can, even now, and if I know them they'd find it more fun to just take the coal and leave us here. That would be nice. Among the many things I am tired of, that coal ranks about second."

Webster's head reared high over Azazel's; it seemed to flatten and spread like a cobra's hood.

"Try it!" he challenged the empty road. "I'm carrying this coal around with me till it hatches, so that makes me a mother, practically. Let them just try taking my young away from me, boy, they'll see some mother love in action. Don't mess with us mothers, boy. Nobody's getting that coal without they stomp my little self to toothpowder."

"Number one among the many things—" Azazel began, but the unicorn interrupted him impatiently.

"Why are they all out after a single coal?" she demanded. "What good will it do them if all the fires are gone?"

"No good at all," Azazel answered airily. "It's just a question of principle. Hell is the home of principle. Always has been." He was plucking up twigs and blades of grass and regarding them with great seriousness. "You might as well go along," he said to the unicorn. "You can't help me."

Hurt and indignant, she said, "I am still proof against hell, surely," but the demon shook his heavy head, slowly as a tolling bell.

"Not this hell, not this year, never again. They'd walk straight over you, with a *by your leave*, and a *don't bother to get up for us*. Your horn has no magic anymore. I can see it fading as I sit here, dying as the coal is dying. Run away now. You can't protect anybody."

Then she turned away from him and started off down the road by herself, although Webster instantly set up a thin yowl of fear and frustration. "Don't leave me!" The wail itself was so eloquently despairing that she could hardly break it up into words. "Don't leave me, don't leave your charming and lovable little buddy," he pleaded, but she broke into an easy trot, feeling as delightfully alone and unhindered as though she were running through her own forest on a cool, new morning, telling herself the story of the time she had met the peculiar demon and traveled with him for a little way. This is what I love, she thought, this is what I am, alone, running. Was it ever any other way? The little wind of her flight soothed her heart and cleared her eyes, making her forget everything but the old sweetness of being herself. *Oh, yes, this is how to be free, whatever the world. This is the way.*

Quite suddenly, the air darkened and thickened about her, hugging hungrily at her feet, seeping into her body, filling her with a cold, heavy fog that seemed to harden inside her and drag her down. She stumbled, broke stride, flailing her neck and floundering in the air as though she were drowning, came at last to a hobbling halt and stood still, breathing very hard and trembling. The spongy air pressed in on her, holding her; the iron taste of it made her cough. She sensed the city.

Actually, the sky remained as clear and soft as ever, and the air that jailed her did not keep the grass from stirring, nor hold a single butterfly still. She could feel a crawling breeze staining her skin wherever it touched her, and yet she knew she was still and white as winter. But she was as sensitive to changes in the air as a bird, as any animal but man, and even a little more than that, because she

was a unicorn. There was no sign of the city where she stood, except for a curl of black smoke a long way off, but she could see it as clearly as if it had swollen out of the ground in front of her eyes, like a savage mirage. She saw the gray streets, and the dark streets, and the streets that were always clean, and she saw high houses and broken houses, and the endless rows of middle-sized houses, grinding like teeth upon the people in the streets. The people were the color of the streets, gray people, dark people, except for a rare flight of children, apple-bright, skittering through the streets like thin rain before the wind. But even as she watched them, she could see them slowing down in the hard air, losing their colors as fish do when they die. She turned her eyes from the children and saw that the city was full of shadows: shadows in doorways, asleep or awake; shadows climbing walls and signs and fences, stepping over gates and watching from rooftops; shadows lying quite still in the streets, waiting for someone who had not come just yet; and shadows going somewhere, slow and sure as alligators. The shadows were darkest in the brightest places—under the lights that hurt the unicorn and reminded her of Azazel's laughter—and it seemed that night and day were happening together in the city, morning in this tree, evening in this room, noon on the blinding sidewalk, midnight between these two people. Through the night and the day, something somewhere in the city pounded and hammered, chattered and screamed like something trying to get out of a burning prison. Its anguish made the whole city shudder before her eyes, made the people in the shivering streets look wildly around for something to attack, something to flee, and made the road sing like a locust under her faraway feet. She could not tell what it was that raged so, nor where it came from—it could have been happening in any of the buildings, or deep under the city; it could even have been the sound made by the thousands of people pushing their way through the air that pushed them back—and in time it made no difference, for it was everywhere and in everyone. It rattled the windows of the houses and made the people inside dance like dust in the sun; it drowned and confused all voices, turning outcries into gummy mumbles and offers of help into stones. The terrible rhythm seized the people by their bones and marched them to and fro, up and down stairs, into little rooms and out of them, back and forth in their houses, around and around in other people's crowded houses; it marched them miles and miles in their beds, it lifted them, set them down, threw them on their backs, lifted them to their feet again and drove them stumbling against one another. It hammered and hammered at the weakest places in them, never giving them time to heal, but only time to invent ways of healing themselves and to buy whatever they told one another could stop the pain.

And the unicorn saw that none of them had any notion of where the pain came from. Whatever it was that screamed in the city had broken its prison long before and invaded them all. It was their screaming now, their own crushing rhythm, and if it had suddenly stopped and they had stood still to hear themselves speaking, to understand what others were saying to them, they would have gone mad with fear instantly, instead of slowly. The rainy smell of their sorrow filled her nostrils, the taste of it choked her throat, and the shiver of it through the road made her body feel as weak and vulnerable as a dead flower. She began to back away.

I don't have to walk through it, she thought dully. I can walk around it, as I walked around all the other cities. But it was too big—it swelled like a soap bubble as she stood watching, blocking the horizon, making the trees within it seem pitiful, ungainly intruders and the clouds above it seem like spies. And she became aware, standing there, that she was already growing numb to the sorrow and the screaming she could feel through the road. There was too much of it for her to understand, too much of it even to feel it all, and it went on forever; there was nothing for her to do but accept it as the best way of living, as each of the marchers in the mirage had done, and she felt it happening to her. Then she became afraid of death, as she never had been in a thousand years, and she turned and started back the way she had come, moving with a clumsy, veering lope as she strained against the air that would have kept her.

Fool, she said to herself, fool, fool, they were always like this, they were like this when they had princes to rule them, they were the same when they came to your forest to hunt you and worship you, they were never any different. They suffer and they spread their suffering, and then they die— how could that have changed? You should not have stayed away from them so long, you should never have come back to them. But she shook herself desperately and stumbled on, crying aloud, "No, it was better before, it was a better time, I know it was." A young man passing by stood looking after her for a long time; an earthworm, who had just seen her go by in the opposite direction, grumbled, "Nobody's ever happy where they are."

Azazel was sitting exactly where she had left him, with Webster's head drooping desolately over his, pleading as mournfully as a honeybird with a deaf bear. The little demon looked up at the sound of her hoofs and yelped with delight, "Little flower, you've come back to me! I knew it, I knew you would, not for a minute did I doubt. We been too much to each other all these years, and then there's the baby—" The unicorn paid no attention to him. She said, "Azazel," but the demon did not raise his head. He sat cross-legged by the road, hunched and silent, and somehow smaller than she remembered, as though the air was wearing him away. How long was I gone, she wondered suddenly, how long was I standing there? She spoke his name again.

"He's playing dead," Webster told her. "He's sitting there and telling himself he's dead." His voice was growing frantic again. "Wind him up again, get him moving," he begged her. "I got to keep going, I got to hang on to that coal, I need it, I got to build with it. They take it away from me, I won't have anything. I'll just sit here with him and play with the grass. Do something, you're such a hotsy-totsy legend. I know my rights, boy. I'm a virgin, so you got to help me, and also I'm practically a mother—"

"Be quiet," she said. "You talk so much, I don't see how you ever got any evildoing done." To Azazel she said, "Listen to me. There is a great city a little further on. Come and see it."

When Azazel answered her at last, his voice was almost a child's voice; light and clear and wonderfully distinct. "Certainly not," he said. "Somebody would come along and sit down in my place. Go away." His eyes had completely lost their yellow menace; they were green now, sunset-green, and very nearly beautiful.

She began to fear, seeing his eyes, that he might actually persuade himself to die, sing himself to sleep in that cold, gentle child's voice. I would be alone then, she thought, and I do not want to be alone. How strange that is, why should it be? I am never afraid or confused when I am by myself, only when I am with others. But I could never walk through that city by myself. How strange, and how stupid, how stupid. If I cannot be alone, how can I live? She had no words for the way she felt, for in all her long life she had never been ashamed.

"I've never seen a city like this," she said to Azazel. "You'll like it."

"Go *away!*" There was a pucker of petulance in the voice now. "I just want to sit here."

"Effendi, you could sit down in the city," Webster broke in eagerly. "You could sit in a park and be a monument, you could sit in a room and be a student. In the winter you could be a snowman, if you wanted, and in the spring, when you melted—"

Azazel moved then, clapping his hands over his ears as desperately as though he really were a snowman trying not to hear himself returning to rain. But the unicorn knew that it was as useless a gesture as hiding his eyes, and she bent her head close to the demon's fingers. "Listen," she said. "The city is like this."

She told him everything she had seen and sensed, leaving out nothing, not the packs of shadows, nor the lights that hurt, nor the cries that made her feel most helpless. At first, he did not want to listen to her; though his body remained motionless, his head lunged and twisted to be away from her, rolling and bobbing like a battered bellbuoy in a high sea. "Leave me alone," he kept whispering, "Let me be," and once, in a voice like the soft scream of a lobster being boiled alive, "*No, you're spoiling—*"; and she, whose whole being was privacy, who had never wanted anything less than to be left alone, baited and tempted him with all the ugliness and sorrow she had seen in the city, to keep him from dying, to keep him from going wherever he wanted to go, to keep from being left alone on the road. I would make a good demon, she thought bitterly, and then: I would make a good human being.

At last, without looking at her, Azazel asked, "How are they with one another?"

"Fearful," she said, and she thought of the few who went mad in small rooms, and of the many who held themselves perfectly still, sipping the air secretly and hoping not to attract anything's attention.

"That's nice," the demon mused. "Then they'll be easy to reach, easy to talk to in a friendly manner, easy to divide from each other and from themselves." He still had not turned to her. "Well, then. Now tell me about their dreams. You are the only creature who could understand and answer me. How are they in their dreams?"

"Scared green," Webster cackled before she could speak. "They wake up running, and they never stop running till it's time to lie down again." His wicked, hopeful face danced and dangled before her eyes, right side up, sideways, upside down, grinning and spinning like the moon gone mad. "They're scareder than we are," he said happily, "which is how come everything."

But the unicorn said, "In their dreams they are brave and loving. Only there."

Azazel did not answer her immediately, and she wondered if even this saddest hope would be enough to keep him sitting by the road with his hands over his ears. But then he turned his face to her, as slowly and suddenly as the night comes, and she saw that the strange green gentleness was gone; the yellow eyes leaped at her and caught her. "Well, that's the best of all," said Azazel. "You can't really have a Hell without dreams of love and bravery and kindness. Not a proper hell, anyway." His eyes were growing brighter every moment as he stared at her.

Webster fidgeted above their heads, constantly glancing back towards the village they had fled. "Come *on*, dad," he grumbled to Azazel. "We get there, we're safe for a little bit. They can't tell themselves from the people anymore." But Azazel sat where he was and held the unicorn with his glowing eyes. His lips began to writhe against each other like eels, shaping an old smile of understanding.

"Of course you had to come back for me," he said pleasantly. "You need me to take you through the city. It's too much like Hell for your crystal heart. You need me." He bit into the words and cracked them between his sharp teeth, smiling at her. She said nothing at all, and the demon's eyes glowed so savagely bright that a ragged company of luna moths, on their way home from a night's revel, fluttered straight into them and sizzled into snowy ashes. Azazel never even blinked.

"Carry me," he said suddenly. "Why should I walk when I have a unicorn to ride? Carry me through the city and we'll see if the people spread palm leaves before us. Carry me, most pure and magic lady, or I'll not move a step to guide you."

There was a terrible comradeship in his smile that the unicorn could not escape, even when she

PETER S. BEAGLE

broke away from his eyes and turned towards the
city again. Before she had taken three steps the
wind brought the sorrowful smell of the city to
her, and then the road began to shiver under her
feet. Still she went on, not walking swiftly, but
not looking back. Behind her, she heard a sigh, a
snicker, a sound like ancient, heavy wings creaking
and rumbling—and then Azazel was limping along
at her shoulder, murmuring, "Well, you don't have
to be rude about it. It's not my fault you lost a little
grace somewhere. It'll make an attractive scar.
Walk slower, my old war wound's acting up." The
little bag of fire gleamed feebly in his left hand, and
Webster swaggered joyously over his head like a
tattered oriflamme.

VI

It took them a much longer time to reach the city than she had imagined, long enough so that the air grew shiny and still with summer and the grass began to turn brown. With Azazel and Webster for company, it was not a particularly terrifying journey: if a distant gasp of pain flashed through her like a needle, Azazel would chant some soothing phrase like *maladjustment*, or *zeitgeist-vulnerable*, or *false value-judgments*; the familiar smell of the murderous clumsiness he made bearable by whispering *unduly complicated interpersonal integrations*. She had no idea what the words meant, but she was glad that human beings at least had names for the sorrows that beset them. Azazel said, yes, it was a help, and laughed softly.

There was no sign of pursuit on their way to the city, although Webster kept yelping warnings at them and urging Azazel to greater speed, and yet there were at least three happenings along the road that made the unicorn certain that they were being followed. Once she chanced to look down and discovered that her feet were leaving tracks in the hard road as deep as if she had been walking in mud. (When she pointed them out to Azazel, whose own goat feet left no prints, he shrugged wearily and said, "Fly.") Again, a scrawny brook, meandering listlessly through a distant meadow, caught sight of them and seemed to discover a purpose in life; it hustled across the field to catch up with them and trailed along beside them for a long time, shining through the wild grass like a snake made of moonlight, before it finally melted into the earth and disappeared. ("Everything rats on you," Webster said, "whatever you are.") And once she heard the voice of the she-demon, soft and undeceived, singing in a grove of trees: *"What is stolen can be found."* ("Yes, I heard her," Azazel said. "What could I do, applaud?") Yet nothing

warned them or menaced them on their journey—
although Webster insisted that the birds' songs
were growing a little threatening—and nothing
sprang out of the night or the dusty afternoon
to bar their way. "They're taking their time," said
Azazel. "Hell does that sometimes."

Once she asked him, "What happened to you
when you were sitting in the grass? Where did you
go?" At first Azazel would not answer at all, but she
pressed him with the patience of an old creature
who is very rarely curious. "What was I spoiling?"
she asked, "and why did you want me to leave you
there?" Webster began to giggle quietly, but he did
not speak.

"I was stopping," Azazel said at last. "That's all.
That's the most a demon can ever hope for, just to
stop, just to be still, not to be, not to move, not to
think, not to mean anything, for good or evil, to let
the machine run down." He spoke so softly that
she could hardly hear him. He said, "Sometimes
a human being gets the most delicate idea of the
machine, and once in a long while one of them even
sees the tiniest part of it, out of the corner of his
eye as it gets someone else. Then they go mad, in
one way or another. Demons have to see the whole

machine, for every single minute that passes, and know it, and be it. To let his part of the machine rundown—that's like a state of grace for a demon. I almost made it once, a long time ago, a very long time. I would have made it, if they'd let me alone."

Webster's laughter spluttered up like fire, full of joyful malice. "You never," he said. "Tell her what really happened, why don't you?" He leaned down to the unicorn, whispering like the fire, "What happened, he got so he thought he was God. Talked himself into it—he believes anything he says, anyway. Oh, he went around stomping and singing and swearing something fierce for a while, yelling, 'I am the Lord, thy God, what I brought you out of the land of Egypt into the Promised Land, so let's have a little respect around here!' And he was running all over writing psalms, and passing miracles right and left—turned a couple of *djinni* into minor prophets, and were never able to get them changed back— and he was damning everybody who sassed him and yelling, 'Depart from me, ye cursed, and watch out besides!' Oh, he was a real terror, boy. Couldn't nobody snap him out of it, neither, and about the time he started looking around for a likely virgin, it got real scary. Finally, he pulled up before Satan's throne, and he went, 'Where wast thou when I laid the foundations of the earth? Declare, if thou hast understanding. Who hath laid the measures thereof, if thou knowest? Or who hath stretched the line upon it? Whereupon are the foundations thereof fastened? . . .'" Webster sighed like a steam engine and patted the balding spot between Azazel's horns. "Went through the whole thing," he said, "behemoth and leviathan and all. There was even a little bit of a whirlwind."

The unicorn imagined Azazel limping amuck among the flametrees and the thorncastles, powerful and frightened, snapping lightning between his fingers and roaring vengeance to assure himself that he could make sounds and be heard. *I wonder if men heard him. I wonder what they thought he was.* "What happened then?" she asked.

"Satan laid him out with a rock," Webster said. "You can't talk fresh to Satan, boy. Not in those days, anyway. Old John the Baptist here was out cold for a couple of centuries." He peered warily at Azazel, ready to flinch away if the other grabbed for him, but Azazel was walking silently along, looking at neither of them. Webster went on thoughtfully, "Satan's always been a little touchy about that Job

PETER S. BEAGLE

business. Says he won. Says it was a moral victory for him, and God knows it. Poor old guy. He ain't got many pleasures in life anymore."

They had walked a long way further without speaking when Azazel gave a little chuckle, sudden and short as the sound of a fish jumping, and said, "Will the unicorn be willing to serve thee, or abide by thy crib? Canst thou bind the unicorn with his band in the furrow? Or will he harrow the valleys after thee? Wilt thou trust him because his strength is great? Or wilt thou leave thy labor to him? Wilt thou believe him, that he will bring home thy seed, and gather it into thy barn?" He spat the words out of his mouth like bones, but they caught the unicorn's ear as anything with her name in it would have done, bones or emeralds.

"Who said that?" she asked hopefully. "Who was talking about me? What does it mean?"

Azazel chuckled again. "He couldn't answer that one either," he murmured. "All he could do was hit. Sore loser."

Afterword
PETER S. BEAGLE

It was 1962, and a lot of things didn't happen. Or hadn't happened quite yet.

The end of the world happened, and then didn't, as Nikita Khrushchev backed down at the last moment and removed Russian nuclear missiles from Cuba. It's generally agreed that—until recently—the world has never again been that close to a planetary duck-and-cover.

President John F. Kennedy hadn't been assassinated yet. That came next year.

Neither had Ngo Dinh Diem, the president of someplace called South Vietnam. That also happened the following year. The Vietnam War hadn't properly happened . . . not exactly, since all we officially had there were "advisors" at the moment. I remember a lot of jokes about advisors that year.

James Meredith didn't get assassinated, as many predicted, when he became the first black student admitted—forcibly—to the University of Mississippi. That strange, brave man wasn't shot until 1963, on his stubbornly solitary walk from Memphis to Jackson, Mississippi. Badly wounded, he survived, unlike James Chaney, Andrew Goodman, Michael Schwerner, Medgar Evers, Viola Liuzzo, and a lot of other people, black and white, in the decade to come.

John Glenn became the first American to orbit the earth.

The Beatles released "Love Me Do."

The grubby little kid people in the Village called Lockjaw Dylan, because half the time you couldn't make out his lyrics, recorded "A Hard Rain's A-Gonna Fall."

The first oral vaccine for polio went on the market.

JFK gave a lot of graduation speeches.

Marilyn Monroe died.

And Phil Sigunick and I rented a cabin in the Berkshires that summer.

It was a guest house, really; the owners lived just down the hill. The mailing address was Cheshire, but the nearest real town was North Adams, where we went on our motorscooters to do our shopping. (I remember a great Polish bakery.) The cabin was remarkably comfortable: we had electricity, running water, a dining table (which also served as a work desk for me), and a serviceable stove. I'm pretty sure we had a telephone . . . or did we go down to the main house, taking advantage of our amiable landlords, to make our calls? Hard to remember, like a lot of things, fifty-seven years later.

We cooked for ourselves, throwing together whatever happened to be in the kitchen: most often Rice-A-Roni, ground meat, maybe some peppers and onions . . . mushrooms when we could get them . . . heavy on the garlic and cumin, and such other spices as smelled interesting. . . . Throw in an egg or two, because why not? Oh, and a certain ground cheese, which I've never found again, and I've hunted for it. We called the whole mess "the good shit."

And in the evenings we played our guitars, for

hours and hours at a time: most often improvising around the music of the great French songwriter Georges Brassens, as well as anything we could steal from our heroes Josh White and Big Bill Broonzy. I usually played rhythm, Phil played lead; we did switch off from time to time, but it was generally understood, "Beagle plays the *bash-bash*, Sigunick does the *deedle-de-dees. . . .*" We listened to a lot of French pop and cabaret that summer—Édith Piaf, of course, and Léo Ferré, and Charles Aznavour, and our beloved sexy Patachou, who discovered Brassens. Back home in the Bronx, we'd play late at one apartment or another, until one set of parents or another threw us out. Here there were no parents, and no traffic, and no phone calls . . . just hours and hours, and being twenty-three in the summer of 1962.

But it was determinedly meant to be a professional summer—and, rather to our mutual amazement, that's actually what it turned out to be. Our days were generally structured around work, with Phil rambling in the beautiful countryside all around us to paint and sketch, and me sitting at the table with my Hermes portable typewriter—a gift from my parents when I set off for college in Pittsburgh—

trying to create . . . something. I'd already published one novel in 1960, then spent a year at Stanford, writing three drafts of a second novel that—like the old English joke about "the curate's egg"—had a few good bits in it. Period. And I had no idea of what to do next.

Or, really, of what kind of writer I was.

I never consciously set out to be an official fantasy writer. That Very Serious Stanford novel was as realistic—if you will—as I could make it, what with a Paris setting, a wandering young man (a musician, though, not a writer), a mysterious older woman with a Past, plenty of love and sex—as best I imagined such things—and even two major gay characters, as precisely observed as I could draw them. A *real* novel . . . not a Bronx ghost story, or whatever it was I'd set off into the world of what Avram Davidson used to call "Liddy-choor" with. A *real* book, such as those reviewed in the *New York Times*, which I drove into North Adams to pick up every Sunday. After all, I knew that I was already ahead of most writers of my age, having both a reputable publisher—the Viking Press—and the legendary agent who had found it for me: my own dear Elizabeth Otis, who was John Steinbeck's agent, and Erskine Caldwell's, and Sinclair Lewis's, and Walker Percy's . . . they wrote *real* books, about real people in real places, not ghosts in Woodlawn Cemetery. And so would I—starting right bloody now, this summer!

Except that nothing happened. Sitting there alone at that perfectly good table, with Phil off investigating the landscape, I made a couple of passes at a couple of different stories—there was one set in Berkeley that had some promise, but didn't go anywhere. . . . And worse, both of them appeared ominously to be fantasies, or were just about to be, any moment I took my eye off them. It wasn't that I didn't like fantasies—*The Wind in the Willows* had been my favorite book since the second or third grade (it probably still is); both Phil and I read a lot of Bradbury and Sturgeon, Poul Anderson and L. Sprague de Camp, and a high-school friend had tipped me off to *The Crock of Gold*, by some Irish guy named James Stephens—but I'd certainly read as much Hemingway and Fitzgerald and Wharton and Dos Passos as anyone in any of my writing classes. These were the real writers, the ones who wrote those real books . . . and I was going to be one of them, *malgré moi*. Whatever the faults of that

Paris novel I'd wasted my Stanford year on, at least it was a real book . . . whatever a real book is. Sixty years, and I've never been entirely sure, except that it's always what someone else is writing.

Always.

So what on earth was I doing, that lovely New England summer morning, sitting at the table with my trusty little typewriter, composing an opening sentence that began, "The unicorn lived in a lilac wood, and she lived all alone." What, exactly, is a lilac wood . . . and for God's sake, what did I have in mind?

I didn't know. I never do. With the exception of my first novel, *A Fine & Private Place*—and, if you will, *The Innkeeper's Song*, my favorite still—I most often make my stories up as they seem to tell themselves, the same way Pooh writes poetry, "letting things come.". I preach heartily against the technique, whenever I'm talking to one writing seminar or another, but it's still what I do, and I put it down personally to laziness. Inspiration has absolutely nothing to do with it. I generally paint myself into a corner, and then pray that my characters—my voices—will talk me free of it. If I can't hear the voices, I'm a lost man. That's just the way it is.

But here was Phil, going out most days with his sketchpad and watercolors (I don't remember any canvases or tubes of paint, but I never knew him without them) and coming back towards evening with work to show—to find me where he'd left me: brooding at the typewriter, most likely, or pacing the room, mumbling to myself, or wandering outside in the sunshine, then wandering back in again. The unicorn lived in a lilac wood, did she? Okay . . . then what? *Think*, schmuck!

I can't speak for Goethe, Tolstoy, or Flaubert, but that's what I've said to myself for my entire career— going all the way back—in bad moments, when I can't hear my voices. I had those two typed words on a dim, dog-eared index card, thumbtacked to my office wall in the barn, until they faded completely from sight. I have them up on this wall now, where I live: printed out now, instead of typewritten. Think, schmuck . . . *think*, damn it. . . .

Okay.

"She was very old, though she did not know it, and she was no longer the careless color of sea foam, but rather the color of snow falling on a moonlit night. But her eyes were still clear and unwearied, and she still moved like a shadow on the sea."

Mmm . . . well, that'll do for the moment, anyway. Although I keep thinking you got that "shadow on the sea" image from somewhere . . . maybe that old Rodgers and Hart song, the way you remember lyrics—all lyrics, good or stupid, in all manner of languages.

So . . . where was I? How should it go now?

"She did not look anything like a horned horse, as unicorns are often pictures, being smaller and cloven-hoofed, and possessing that oldest, wildest grace that horses have never had, that deer have only in a shy, thin imitation and goats in dancing mockery. . . ."

For someone who had always been attracted and allured by unicorns since childhood, I really didn't know much to write about them in the summer of 1962. I had come across Dorothy Lathrop's story *The Colt from Moon Mountain* almost as soon as I could read to myself . . . and there was a family legend that I had, at the age of four or so, spent a morning sitting in front of my mother's elementary-school class, telling them unicorn stories.

When it was time to leave, apparently I stood up and said, "Goodbye. I'll come back sometime, and tell you more about unicorns." That's the way my mother always told it to my aunts and uncles . . . and I sure wish to hell I could remember whatever I had in mind back then.

"Unicorns are immortal. It is their nature to live alone in one place: usually a forest where there is a pool clear enough for them to see themselves—for they are a little vain, knowing themselves to be the most beautiful creatures in all the world, and magic besides. . . . The last time she had seen another unicorn the young virgins who still came seeking her now and then had called to her in a different tongue—but then she had no idea of months or years or centuries, or even of seasons. It was always spring in her forest, because she lived there. . . ."

In 1962, if you wanted to look something up, you went to the library. I still do, even though I've learned my way around Wikipedia and a small—*very* small—handful of assorted useful websites. But I've loved libraries all my life, ever since I discovered that that's where the books live. The only one I knew within range of Cheshire was in Pittsfield, where I'd once spent a summer with my family. I hopped on Margot (my scooter's name was Margot, after the girl in Georges Brassens' song "Brave Margot"), and set off.

I was looking specifically for a book by Odell Shepard called *The Lore of the Unicorn*. Published in the 1930s, it had been long out of print in 1962, but today it's easily available, probably even at the Pittsfield Public Library. Back then, the only information it had on unicorns in its entire catalogue was a reference to one Dr. Olfert Dapper, who had seen a wild unicorn in the Maine woods in 1673. The article didn't say that he claimed to have seen a unicorn, or was reported to have seen a unicorn; it was a definite statement, and that was all there was to it. I took that as an omen, and determined that I would dedicate *The Last Unicorn*—at least in part—to Dr. Dapper. If I ever got the damn thing finished.

As always, I was making the damn thing up as I went along. The story was originally conceived—as far as I conceived any of it—as a sort of James Thurber–esque self-aware fairytale spoof, employing traditional fairytale characters like unicorns, witches, outlaws, wicked kings, and kindly princes—and then to do something very else with them. I believe they call that sort of thing metafiction today. (I hadn't read Angela Carter then, and anyway, she's special.) It's perfectly legitimate, but it's tricky work, and you can only get away with it if you're a born satirist. I'm not, but I didn't know that then.

The beginning moved briskly enough, and I actually felt myself settling easily into my stride—until the dragon showed up. The Butterfly, who came later, is, in the book and the movie, the creature who informs the unicorn that she is the solitary survivor of her people. In that first draft, however, she receives the news from a dragon: a battered, harassed dragon, who has been through an exhausting, frustrating encounter with modern times, and, brought to tears by the unicorn's invitation to battle, is now crawling back into the forest to die. I was fond of him—he has some really good lines—but I don't remember any special difficulty, or any artistic qualms, in replacing him with the Butterfly. (Though I was quite happy to see him reappear, many years later, in my story "Oakland Dragon Blues." It did seem only proper.)

But the Butterfly now . . .

I've called him a self-portrait many times, over many years. The reason for this is that—with one or two important exceptions—he can only speak in quotations, whether from great literature, old movies, songs of every vintage and quality, radio commercials, or the strange private jokes that Phil and I were cracking ourselves up with in the summer of 1962. ("You don't get no medal" is the punch line of the mildly dirty one about Queen Elizabeth and Prince Philip.) We spoke—and still do, fifty-seven years later—a language evolved out of a combination of old vaudeville routines, a lot of Hope and Crosby, classic Jewish jokes, a great deal of Pogo-talk (whole Sunday comic-strip pages learned by heart), and simply having lived across the street from each other since we were five years old. It's all there in the Butterfly's speech, (which took me three days to write), and today I can't always explain, even to myself, where some of those lines came from. But I can definitely tell you that "Your name is a golden bell hung in my heart . . . ." is from the Brian Hooker translation of *Cyrano de Bergerac*, and the following quotation, "I would break my body to pieces to call you once by your name. . . ." is from Stephen Vincent Benet's lovely small poem to his wife, whose name was Rosemary. People ask about those two lines.

And it's the Butterfly, in both versions, who first mentions the mysterious and deadly Red Bull to the unicorn. The Bull is the other element in the story which people ask to have explained, and I've never been able to tell them any more than, "I don't know. He was just *there*." There's a Brown Bull who was the cause of a legendary Irish war—and there's a bull from the sea in Mary Renault's retelling of the Greek epic of Theseus—and Kipling's Kim is told to seek a red bull on a green field to find his British father's regiment . . . maybe that's where I got the terrible beast's color? Oh, I can describe him well enough, from his first appearance, because I make things up. But for the rest of it—and this includes anything I may have said about the Red Bull, ever—that damn Butterfly told me everything I know about him. "*They passed down all the roads long ago, and the Red Bull ran close behind them, and covered their footprints. . . .*" That's it. That's all. And I'm grateful.

But there is no Schmendrick in that first version of the tale—and no Molly Grue, the true heart of *The Last Unicorn*. No Molly . . . no book, as I should have realized far earlier than I did. What there is is a two-headed demon named Azazel. That's the proper name of the first head, who looks like an ancient Babylonian deity, and is a genuinely impressive personage. The second head exists on the end of a long, snaky neck, sprouting from somewhere between Azazel's shoulders. That's Webster. The unicorn doesn't meet him right away.

Azazel and Webster talk a great deal like Phil and me—especially as we talked when we were young and took real joy in snapping and snarking at each other. Take the classic *Pogo* line, "I was beginnin' to like havin' you for a enemy, but now I'm beginnin' to remember why I hated havin' you for a friend!" We can still talk that talk today, falling into those rhythms effortlessly: Albert the Alligator and Pogo Possum forever, changing off roles just as we traded licks on our guitars . . . but the roles were fresher then, I suppose, the improvisations perhaps a bit more loaded with surprises and sudden, eager delights.

These days, if we're not awfully careful, we find ourselves talking almost like grown-ups . . . and God pity the pair of us then. Almost eighty or not (Phil's three months younger than I am), we have no business talking like grown-ups, not to each other. Even Phil's children know better than that.

Azazel is a traditionalist, greatly distressed and implacably angered by the fact that Hell has gone modern, replacing the good old eternal contracts signed in blood and filed away in proper grand cabinets, with computers and cloud-storage. (At least they would have done, if I'd known anything about computers in that summer of 1962. Not many people did then, this side of the CIA.)

Webster, on the other hand, is an anarchist, pure and simple. That's all that really needs to be said about Webster. He's in favor of blowing things up, whether modern or old-style, just on general principles. It was Webster who blew up as much of the new McHell as he could reach, setting himself and Azazel on the road, in fateful possession of a single coal from the remaining eternal flames. With all Hell following after.

Once again, remember that I was making all this up as I went along, usually alone in that comfy little cabin, with Phil off doing painterly stuff—and most often coming home with something to show for his day's work—while I struggled and invented, and crossed out (no *delete* buttons on typewriters) and tried again. I told you—that's what I do.

So . . . the unicorn accepts Azazel and Webster as companions on the road, because why not? Journeys are lonely—especially if you're never been on a journey before—and there's at least something to be said for associating with immortal creatures like yourself. Their first pursuer—there were meant to be others—is a beautiful, nameless demon who frightens the hell (so to speak) out of Azazel, and who sings what eventually became Mommy Fortuna's song, *"What is gone is gone. . . ."* But I hadn't met Mommy Fortuna then. Or Schmendrick and Molly, as I've said . . . or my dear, hopeless Captain Cully. They were all in the wind still—like me. Very much like me.

I was Snoopy on his doghouse roof—*"Suddenly a shot rang out! A maid-servant screamed! A pirate ship appeared on the horizon!"*—and that particular road will only take you so far. Which I never learn, no matter how long I've been on that road. No matter how inventive with plot you are, no matter how dexterous with dialogue . . . sooner or later, not knowing what the hell you're doing *will* catch up with you. In my case, it took me—and this first raw attempt at *The Last Unicorn*—all summer.

Oh, there's more stuff. The unicorn and the ancient demon with the two constantly quarrelling heads travel through a strange, cold city—unnamed, but I'm sure I had Kafka in mind—with the forces of Hell close behind, in pursuit of that single stolen coal. Azazel is determined to win to safety in order to start up a private, copyrighted, traditional hell of his own: a decent Gehenna, staffed by demons who can be induced to give up distressed jeans, Hawaiian shirts and Disney-character tattoos, and get back into proper horns and tails. Any number of real satirists, from Max Beerbohm to Saki to Charles G. Finney and Evelyn Waugh, all the way to the entire writing staff of *Monty Python*, or their classic ancestor, *The Goon Show*, could have done something good with that idea. I couldn't.

And that's how I find things out, by doing them wrong, giving up on them, and sometimes— *sometimes*—coming back to them, and in time beginning to understand what I did wrong. I may not be able to fix them, even then—understanding isn't the same as getting it right—but I never throw them away. Never. Because, as Fats Waller always said, "One never know, do one?"

So. Come September, Phil and I emptied the refrigerator, finishing up the last of "the good shit," loaded the motorscooters (we had to do a last-minute ring job on Brave Margot, propped upside down on Phil's bed), and raced each other back to the Bronx.

The next spring, far too early for the weather, we set off for California together . . . but that's another journey on another couple of scooters (their names were Jenny and Couchette), and, as it turned out, another book—a book about that journey, called *I See By My Outfit*, which remains the most fun I've ever had writing a book. They *can* be fun. . . .

And I put *The Last Unicorn* aside for a long while. I learned to write magazine pieces, primarily for the late, much-lamented *Holiday* magazine (they serialized *I See By My Outfit* in advance of its publication), which put bread on the table and taught me the freelance trade. I had a family to feed by then, and bills to pay, the only way I knew, and no time at all for unicorns and butterflies. For the first time in my life, I was a working man.

I kept *The Last Unicorn* in a deep-down desk drawer, never thinking about it—or even looking at it—even into the crazy time, the full-tilt Governor Reagan 1960s, when the two Santa Cruz FBI guys came trudging wearily up my muddy dirt road on a fairly regular basis, to ask about whichever student revolutionary had stayed over last weekend to wash the tear gas out of his eyes. They never expected an answer, but we always gave them coffee.

But I had assignments to learn to deal with (everything from covering a cockfight at a ranch outside Healdsburg to a voting-rights campaign in Somerville, Tennessee), and a precarious living to make at my "craft or sullen art." And I had three children to tell bedtime stories to every night. They especially liked the tales about the misadventures of the world's worst magician . . . the one with the funny name.

Gradually, cautiously, dubiously, I began to steal time between rent-paying gigs to mess with *The Last Unicorn* once more. It remained the nightmare it always was—that never changed, except for the pure pleasure of writing the incidental lyrics—but by the time the bloody thing at last got rolling for real, with Schmendrick, Molly, King Haggard, Prince Lir, and Captain Cully aboard, I was supposed to be working on a book about California for a different publisher. There was a due date, and there had been an advance. I will always bless Michael Bry, the photographer I'd been traveling all over the state with for a year, who constantly reassured the publisher that I was constantly taking extensive notes on our journey, and would be providing the words to accompany his striking pictures ("developing Peter's head," as he put it) any day now. It's impossible to be certain, after fifty years, but I *think* I handed in the text for *The California Feeling* about six weeks after the unicorns came out of the sea. Something like that.

So. Here's the way the unicorn started her journey, on a summer afternoon in a little house on a green hill, with the guitars propped in the far corner.

About the Author

Peter Soyer Beagle is the internationally best-selling and much-beloved author of numerous classic fantasy novels and collections, including *The Last Unicorn, Tamsin, The Line Between, Sleight of Hand, Summerlong, In Calabria,* and most recently, *The Overneath.* He is the editor of *The Secret History of Fantasy* and the co-editor of *The Urban Fantasy Anthology.*

Beagle published his first novel, *A Fine & Private Place,* at nineteen, while still completing his degree in creative writing. Beagle's follow-up, *The Last Unicorn*, is widely considered one of the great works of fantasy. It has been made into a feature-length animated film, a stage play, and a graphic novel. He has written widely for both stage and screen, including the screenplay adaptations for *The Last Unicorn* and the animated film of *The Lord of the Rings*, and the well-known "Sarek" episode of *Star Trek*.

As one of the fantasy genre's most-lauded authors, Beagle is the recipient of the Hugo, Nebula, Mythopoeic, and Locus awards as well as the Grand Prix de l'Imaginaire. He has also been honored with the World Fantasy Life Achievement Award and the Inkpot Award from the Comic-Con convention, given for major contributions to fantasy and science fiction.

Beagle lives in Richmond, California.

About the Artist

Stephanie Law's work is an exploration of mythology mixed with her personal symbolism. Her art journeys through surreal otherworlds, populated by dreamlike figures, masked creatures, and winged shadows. In her early career, she worked with various fantasy game, magazine, and book publishers as an illustrator. She created the Shadowscapes Tarot, a best-selling deck that has been translated into more than a dozen languages, and is the author of the series of watercolor technique books *Dreamscapes*.

She currently focuses on working with galleries for showcasing her personal work, and with botanical gardens and environmental organizations for her botanical art, while continuing to publish projects like her recent art book, *Descants & Cadences*, which features her aesthetics of mythos woven with movement and the natural world, and *Succulent Dragons*, which combines her love of the intricate patterns of nature and whimsical fantastical creatures.

Law lives in the San Francisco Bay Area.